PAINTED LOVE

LACY EMBERS

HIDDEN KEY PUBLISHING

CHAPTER 1

The best part about going to clubs was there was no talking.

Leticia let the bass rumble up through the floor and through her body until she was shaking with it, vibrating, left with no choice but to dance along. She could feel her heart thumping in time with the beat, turning her very pulse into an extension of the music. This was what she was good at: the electric bang-bang-slide, the magnetic pull of bodies, the thrill of touching a stranger.

She moved through the crowd, grinding up against one person, then partnering with another. All week she'd waited for Friday to come. The tension had been building up in between her shoulder blades for days.

When she'd been approached about the promotion, her only thought had been excitement. Head curator for a leading museum? It was her dream. There were technicalities to deal with, especially since it had taken her so long to get her PhD, but the museum wanted to give her time to prepare... She'd been so excited that she hadn't even thought about all the extra work it would be.

Now she knew, and she had to work this tension out. She'd been staying late all week, sometimes until ten at night. Sharon had already suggested that Leticia was overworking herself. Work hard, play hard

—that had always been her motto. But now the work was outweighing the play and that simply wouldn't do. Time to play until she forgot everything else, forgot everything except for the music and the feel of someone's hands on her.

One song was just finishing and moving, slick and perfect, into another song, when she felt a new kind of vibration. Her phone was ringing.

Leticia sighed and fought her way off of the dance floor. Pulling her phone out of her pocket, she saw Sharon's name flash across the screen.

Ah, guilt. The feeling that makes the world go 'round.

"Hey!" She yelled, grabbing a seat at the bar. "What's shaking?"

"You, I presume," Sharon replied. "I can barely hear you. Where are you?"

"A club. Where else?" Leticia replied.

It was difficult to hear anything over the pounding music, but she knew her best friend well enough to know by now when Sharon was sighing at her. "So Ross and I might be late for Melanie and Tom's birthday tomorrow. I was hoping you could pick up the cake?"

"You couldn't text me about this?"

"You're terrible at answering texts when you're at a club. You'll sleep in way too late tomorrow, especially if you pick up a guy, and by the time you saw the text it'd be too late."

"Fair point." Speaking of finding a guy... Leticia scanned the crowd. There were plenty of gorgeous men out there tonight. She smiled to herself. "All right, send me the address and I'll pick it up."

"You're the best. Thanks! Have fun and be safe. Don't do anyone I wouldn't do!"

"So, you want me to steal your husband. Gotcha."

"Real funny. I'll see you tomorrow. Love you!"

"See you then. Love you, too!"

Leticia disconnected the call just as a man slid up to the bar. Her eyes widened a little and she swiveled around to get a better look at him.

Well, hello, gorgeous. Leticia bit her lip. Talk about your all-American male. Tall, well-built, and tan with blonde hair just long enough for her to muss up and tangle her fingers in.

She laid her fingertips on his arm. "'Scuse me," she said. "Mind if I buy you a drink?"

The guy turned and smiled at her and Leticia melted just a little bit inside. He belonged on the cover of a magazine or something. His shirt was sticking to him a little from sweat, so she could see the outline of his muscles underneath. She wanted to climb him like a tree. "Isn't that usually my line?" He asked.

"What can I say, I'm a bit of a rebel," Leticia replied. She signaled the bartender.

"I probably shouldn't drink, actually," the guy admitted. "I'm here for my friend's bachelor party and everyone's already pretty smashed."

"You playing designated driver?"

"Somebody's got to make sure they don't do anything stupid," the man pointed out.

"That's real responsible of you..." Leticia trailed off.

"Carter," he replied. He held out his hand for her to shake.

It made her laugh, but she shook it anyway. "I'm Leticia." His hand was warm around hers. "If you don't want a drink, then, how about a dance?"

Carter glanced further down the bar, probably where his friends were. Leticia slid off the barstool and up against him, placing a hand on his chest. "C'mon," she purred. She knew what that purr did to men. "They won't burn the place down if you dance for a couple of songs, will they?"

"I suppose not," Carter admitted.

Leticia winked at him, taking his hand and leading him out onto the dance floor.

It didn't take her long to find a rhythm, and she rocked back into Carter, fitting her ass back against him. She felt him stiffen in surprise, but then he relaxed and put his hands at her hips. "You don't get out much, do you?" She asked, leaning back against him so that he could hear her.

"Not really." Then Carter slid an arm around her waist to pull her even closer and ducked his head down to nose at the side of her neck. "Doesn't mean I don't know how this works, though."

Leticia let herself move into him more, the beat setting the pace. Soon they were moving together, Carter's arm a heavy weight anchoring her, keeping her pinned to him. She moved her hips, circling them, shoving them back, until she could feel Carter start to harden behind her.

"Mm, looks like you do know how this works," she told him.

She had no idea how long they danced like that. Carter kept an arm around her waist and his other hand at her thigh, high up enough to tease. Her head was back against his shoulder and she could feel every inch of him. She wanted his hand up higher, right between her legs, where she was getting wet. She wanted his mouth on hers. She wanted to feel his skin.

Fortunately, Leticia was never the type to not take what she wanted. She spun around to face front, then pressed herself all the way up against him.

Carter growled and hauled her up against him, sliding his thigh in between her legs. She ground down against him and the pressure sent heat ricocheting through her. Leticia moaned, doing it again, and again. She looped her arms around his neck and Carter hauled her up closer to him, bringing a hand down to cup her ass and skimming his lips over her throat.

"You look gorgeous like this," Carter marveled, his mouth right at her ear. He jolted his thigh, rubbing the fabric of his jeans right up against her clit. Leticia gasped, her entire body giving a spasm at the pleasure. Carter gave a mischievous chuckle. "Did you like that?"

He did it again and Leticia moaned. Again, and again, until she felt dizzy and lightheaded.

"I wonder if you could come just like this," Carter marveled, his voice sounding like he was in awe.

Leticia could feel him hard against her leg and laughed, tugging his mouth to hers. "Like you're not dying yourself," she replied, just before sealing her mouth over his.

Carter gave a groan that she could feel vibrating against her chest, his tongue sliding into her mouth. Leticia shuddered against him as he sucked and licked at her. His hands kept roaming her body, bunching up her dress, while his leg kept thrusting up against her. It would be so easy to get off like this, writhing on Carter's leg until her body shook in ecstasy, but she didn't want that. She'd done that plenty of times in clubs, but not for tonight. It was rare that she saw someone as handsome, someone she wanted as badly, as Carter. She wanted all of him. Not just rubbing one off together amongst a crowd.

Leticia slid her hand into his hair, tugging on the soft strands until she could tilt his head away from her mouth and get her lips to his ear. "There's a back room," she told him. "C'mon."

She slid away from him, grabbing his hand to lead him. Carter seemed a little stunned but he let her lead him through the crowd. It wasn't easy. Everywhere, bodies pressed up against them. But she'd done this before, many times, and she knew the way. It took far too long to get back to someone's apartment. Besides, it never paid to be cautious—she didn't exactly want a guy she didn't know coming back to her place. Just in case.

The guy who owned the club had created a small back room for when he wanted a little privacy. Leticia had used it before, and had found it perfectly fitting for a little fun. She didn't want to use it often in case the owner got mad, but she was on pretty good terms with him, and he had told her about the room, after all, so she figured— every once in a while, what's the harm?

Leticia reached the back wall of the club, over to the side away from the DJ's stage. There was a thick red curtain but no bouncer there. Good, that meant the owner, Jeremy, wasn't using the room tonight.

Carter crowded up behind her, his hands falling to her hips. He pressed a few kisses up along the side of her neck and Leticia paused, her head falling back to give him better access. For someone who didn't do this much, he was damn good at it.

"That's not a bathroom or supply closet or something, is it?" Carter asked, his tone dry and humorous.

Leticia laughed. Once upon a time it would have been but, despite how much she loved going out, she wasn't twenty-one anymore. "Nope. Just you wait."

Carter made an impatient, growling noise against her neck and Leticia's knees went a little weak. She forced herself to pull away before she did something regrettable, like take him right there on the dance floor in front of strangers. She'd seen other people doing that before, caught glimpses of it in clubs, but she was never the type for that. She didn't like an audience.

She pulled aside the curtain, revealing a heavy door with a keypad. She grinned to herself and quickly dialed the four-digit code to swing the door open.

"You're a regular deviant, aren't you?" Carter said. He sounded equal parts concerned and delighted.

Leticia wasn't sure what to do with someone who was like this— one half of him eager and ready to make her come on the dance floor, the other half hesitant and bewildered like he couldn't quite believe this was happening. It was kind of adorable.

"I'm a lot of things," she told him, leading him into the room and closing the door behind him. The door hadn't been there originally, just the curtain, until one too many couples had gotten interrupted and the owner had installed the door. As far as Leticia knew, she was the only one in the club tonight who knew the code. She hadn't seen any other regulars.

So much the better for her.

The inside of the room was simple. It had low lighting and was done up in red, with a sort of small stage in the middle, on which was a pole. That had been put in about two years ago after some crazy night that Jeremy still wouldn't tell Leticia about, but it apparently involved a lot of tequila. Surrounding the stage were large, plush couches, also in red.

There really wasn't any doubt about what this room was used for. Leticia ignored the pole—she'd always wanted to learn but still hadn't found the time—and instead lay down on one of the couches. They were conveniently large enough for her to spread out on her back, like a bed.

She smiled up at Carter. The dark, heated look in his eyes made her shiver.

"It's kind of hard to be a deviant alone," Leticia told him, using that purr again. She stroked her fingers up her inner thigh as she said it, letting her legs spread.

Carter moved so fast she couldn't even see it. One moment he was standing over her, and the next he was pinning her to the couch. His hands braced on either side of her head and he leveraged himself down, kissing her deeply. Leticia moaned. She'd always loved the feeling of a strong man pinning her down. She squirmed, letting him fall between her legs, just so she could feel how real the weight of him was above her, how much pressure he put on her body.

She wrapped her legs around him and arched against him. Carter groaned and ground down against her. It was like on the dance floor, but better, the full weight of him bearing down on her.

"I want you inside of me," she admitted, sliding her hands up underneath his shirt to feel his hard muscles. They didn't give when she pushed, solid and unyielding, and she shivered delightedly.

"You—" Carter started, and then cut himself off with a frustrated noise. "If you keep saying things like that, I'm not going to be held responsible for my actions."

"Then don't be," Leticia replied, challenging him. She nipped at his jaw. "C'mon, I want to forget my own name."

That was why she came to these places, after all: to dance and drink and fuck until she forgot all of the problems and worries her day job brought.

Carter gave her a sly smile and slid a hand down to cup her breast, his thumb swiping over one of her nipples. "I think I can manage that."

He kissed her again and Leticia let him, her hands sliding all over him, trying to touch every party of him that she could reach. She felt greedy, but Carter definitely didn't mind, judging by the pleased little growls that he made. His large hands moved down her body, pushing her dress up until he could touch her stomach and the underside of her breasts. Her dress might as well have been off, for all the covering it was doing.

"Nothing underneath?" Carter asked, sounding pleased and predatory.

Leticia shook her head. "Can't wear a bra with this dress, I've never been comfortable dancing in a thong, and any other kind of underwear ruins the line of the dress."

"Or, you're just a little minx who knew what she was coming here for," Carter pointed out.

Leticia laughed and winked at him. "That too."

Carter moved his hands so they were at her ass and between her shoulder blades, and then Leticia felt him lifting her. She gave an instinctive little squeak, tightening her legs around him, as he rolled them and sat up, putting her firmly in his lap.

Leticia panted into his mouth, feeling him pressing up between her legs. She wanted him inside of her so badly, it felt like her brain was short-circuiting. "Please," she gasped, pressing kisses into his face and neck.

"Patience is a virtue," Carter said, but he undid his belt and jeans and shimmed them off as Leticia obligingly lifted her hips to give him the room.

She licked her lips. Part of her wanted to slide down to her knees and get her mouth on him for a little while, but she also didn't know if she could wait that long.

Carter tugged down the top of her dress, exposing her breasts. Leticia realized what he was going to do just a second before he did it, and she only had time to tangle her fingers in his hair before he latched his mouth onto one of her nipples.

Heat shot through her, straight to her core, and she could feel herself getting even wetter. Carter scraped his teeth lightly along her skin and she keened, hips bucking. She wanted him to never stop, but she also wanted this madness to end. Writhing on his lap, he was almost inside of her—close, but not quite enough.

Carter's hand came up to play with her other breast, his free hand still at her back, keeping her trapped on his lap. Leticia clawed at his back, the double sensation driving her insane. His shirt wasn't even off and here she was, dress technically on but covering nothing, sobbing with frustration and arousal on his lap. God, she loved this.

"God, you're gorgeous," Carter whispered, finally pulling away. The hand at her breast slid down between her legs and she felt his thumb pressing, searching, until it found her clit. She jolted, pleasure spiking up in her, and she moaned helplessly.

"Please," she begged. "Please, please—"

He rubbed at her for a minute, merciless, fast and just a little rough, exactly how she liked it. Her head fell forward onto his shoulder and she moaned over and over again, her hips jerking helplessly. She could feel Carter's mouth at her neck, panting hotly in her ear and, she was so close to coming, she could taste it in the back of her throat.

"Tell me you have protection," she gasped. "I want—I want you so bad, please, tell me you have something—"

"Hold on, beautiful," Carter said, the hand at her back rubbing up and down soothingly. His hand slid away from her and she almost screamed in frustration, but then his fingers were at her lips.

"Go on," he told her. "Suck."

Leticia felt a gut-punch of arousal hit her and she took his fingers into her mouth, tasting herself on him. She moaned, both at the sensation and at the way Carter watched her, his pupils blown wide and his face tight with desire.

Then he ducked his head down. There was a rustling sound, and a moment later he sat straight back up again, condom in hand.

"These were for my friends," Carter admitted. He sounded a little sheepish and Leticia bit down slightly on his fingers, teasing him. He rolled his eyes at her, but in a fond sort of way. "Deviant."

He withdrew his fingers and Leticia quipped, "Takes one to know one."

Carter laughed and, without any warning, slid a finger inside of her. Leticia gasped and shuddered. It was teasing but not enough, not nearly enough to fill her up the way that she wanted. "That's it," Carter said, adding a second finger. "Make those little noises for me."

Leticia didn't bother trying to hide the gasps and moans she made, and then he added a third finger and all she could do was make little *ah, ah, ah,* noises. It really wasn't the best angle but she'd need to turn around for that and she couldn't move if her life had depended on it. This was fine, this was good enough, teasing and rough.

"I'm ready," she promised. "Please, I need it."

Carter didn't even have a quip to say to that. He just closed his eyes and let out a kind of helpless groan. His fingers moved out of her and Leticia couldn't help but whimper a bit at the loss of them. But she raised her hips up obligingly and heard the rip of the condom wrapper. A moment later, Carter's hands were at her hips.

"Go slow if you need to," he told her. Then he was guiding her down onto him.

Leticia felt a scream get strangled at the back of her throat as she sank down onto his length. He wasn't the longest she'd ever had but, by God, he just might be the thickest. It felt like he was stretching her impossibly wide and she loved it, ached for it, wriggling to take more of him inside of her. It gave her a pleasant burn, pleasure with a sharp edge of almost-pain.

Carter was breathing heavily, his eyes glued to the spot where they were joined, his jaw clenched. Leticia rolled her hips experimentally, testing how it felt, and Carter's head fell back against the wall with a thunk.

"You like that?" Leticia asked, teasing, rolling her hips again.

Carter grit his teeth, his cock jerking inside of her. "You're so tight, God—"

Leticia hummed, rolling her hips again, getting herself comfortable enough with him inside to start moving up and down on him. "You feel so good, filling me up like this," she said. "I feel stretched so wide, it's amazing. I want you to fuck me like this until I'm screaming, until I can't even move, I just have to let you give it to me. Fuck me until I'm helpless."

Carter grabbed her, hauling her even closer to him, and *there.* Leticia cried out, pressure back on her clit, and her entire body shuddered in pleasure. Carter got a determined look on his face. "Whatever you want," he promised her, and then he started thrusting up into her.

He didn't start slow or gentle, just set a rough, demanding pace that had her thighs trembling in no time. She clawed at his back, ecstasy getting pushed into her with every thrust. It felt like she was getting split wide open and she couldn't get enough of it. She knew she was babbling, saying things like *yes* and *Oh God, more, harder,* but it all sounded dim and distant underneath the roaring in her ears.

She started thrusting down onto him, but it wasn't long before her entire body was twitching and all she could do was drape herself over him and let him fuck hard and fast up into her. Her body felt like it was on fire, each thrust making her jerk and spasm. It was good, so good, and she knew she wasn't even going to need any extra help to come.

Carter started making more aborted thrusts, losing his rhythm, and she knew he was close. Leticia turned her head, biting down lightly on his shoulder. "That's it," she gasped. "That's it, fuck, come inside me, just like that!"

Carter tightened his grip on her and she felt his cock jerk inside of her as he came and oh, fuck, that was it, that was what she'd needed. She bit his shoulder again, harder this time, shaking uncontrollably as sparks flew behind her eyes. It felt almost like her orgasm was ripped out of her, pleasure tangled with just a hint of pain, robbing her of her breath.

"Oh no," Carter panted. "I'm not done with you yet."

He pulled out of her and she whimpered, but then she was being maneuvered to lie down on the couch. Carter spread her legs and she looked down at him. He gave her a wicked grin. "I want to hear you scream for me."

Leticia all but melted at the sinful tone in his voice, and then he was ducking his head between her legs and licking at her and she really did melt. Her whole body went boneless and she gripped at the couch, trying to find purchase. Carter was relentless, running his tongue through her folds and then lapping at her clit. He wasn't even giving her a chance to breathe. Her first orgasm wasn't even truly finished and already she could feel the second one building up inside of her. It felt like drowning, gasping a breath only to be plunged underneath the water again. She loved it.

Then he added two fingers, crooking them up inside of her, and she started to scream.

"There it is," Carter said, pulling away just long enough to press a kiss to her inner thigh before diving back in again.

He seemed to know right when she was about to come again, because he would pull away and stroke his hands down her legs, pressing soft, lingering kisses into the soft skin until she had calmed down a bit. He kept doing it, again and again, until Leticia thought she didn't even know what time was anymore. Everything was gone, narrowed down just to her own pleasure, the orgasm she needed so badly.

"Please," she choked out. Her voice felt rubbed raw from all of the screaming—and she had been screaming, and whimpering, and pleading, just like Carter had wanted.

Carter didn't say anything. He just smiled at her. But that was all the answer she needed. When he ducked his head back down between her legs she was already anticipating it. He swirled his tongue around her and sucked, hard, his fingers crooking up deep inside of her, and she couldn't have held it in if she tried.

Leticia could honestly say that she'd never come so hard in her life. She could feel tears starting to leak out of the corner of her eyes. It felt so good, so very, very, good. She couldn't stop shaking, each tremor only sending more pleasure through her. It was equal parts exhausting and exhilarating.

By the time she started to become aware of her surroundings again, she didn't think she could have moved even if she'd wanted to. Her limbs felt unbearably heavy. Her head felt like it was floating, detached from the rest of her.

"Holy fuck," Carter said, his voice hoarse. "You're making me wish I was ten years younger."

Leticia tried to laugh, but it came out as a tired, sighing chuckle. "Best club hookup ever," she admitted playfully.

"Oh good, I'd hate to be only second best," Carter teased. He crawled up her body, finally pulling his shirt off. Leticia ran her hands over the broad, lightly tanned chest.

"What are you, a gym instructor or something?" She asked. Damn, the guy seemed to be made of solid muscle. Not that she was complaining.

Carter chuckled. "Nothing like that. I was a huge bookworm growing up, so to keep people from beating me up I started working out. So I could hold my own, y'know? And then I found that I liked it. It helps take my mind off the day."

"See when I want to do that..." Leticia nipped at his lower lip. "I go to a club."

"Ah, the continual struggle between introverts and extroverts," Carter said with an exaggerated sigh.

Leticia thought for a moment. She didn't want the night to end. She wanted to get Carter properly naked and to take her time with him. She didn't normally invite men back to her place, but... if Carter was the kind of guy she should be concerned about, she had a feeling he'd be showing signs of it by now. Instead he just seemed like an oddly sweet guy who knew what he was doing in the bedroom.

And dammit, she'd just gotten a promotion. She deserved to treat herself.

"Would you like to go back to my place?" She asked.

Carter's eyebrows rose up. He looked surprised. "Are you sure?"

"It's not something I make a habit of," Leticia admitted. "But I don't like the idea of this evening ending so soon, do you?"

Carter looked a little conflicted, so she looped her arms around his waist and started kissing his chest. "Your friends will be fine. Isn't the whole point of a bachelor party to have everyone do crazy things?"

"I suppose that's fair." Carter pulled her back up so they could lock eyes. "And I'm not done with you, either."

Leticia shivered delightedly.

Carter found his friends and told them he'd be heading out while Leticia cleaned herself up and got her car from the valet. The ride back to her apartment was pretty quiet, but surprisingly not uncomfortable. That was another reason she'd always avoided bringing guys back to her place. She never knew what to say to them on the way there, and it just felt awkward. She was good with actions, not so much with words.

But this was nice. Carter kept his hand on her leg the whole time, tracing idle patterns with his fingers. The mood was anticipatory without being too jittery. Maybe it was the fact that she'd already orgasmed—twice.

She shivered again. Damn but that man knew how to touch a woman. She couldn't wait to get him into a proper bed.

Leticia rather liked her apartment. It was a tiny studio that she'd gotten years ago, back when she'd first landed her job at the museum. Sharon had always been telling her that it was high time she moved into a nicer place, but Leticia hadn't seen any reason to. Why would she when she was hardly ever home? She spent more time at the museum or at Sharon and Ross's place than she did at her apartment anyway. She'd move when the time was really right, like when she was moving in with a guy.

Like that was ever going to happen at this rate, but whatever. She loved her job and so what if it hadn't left her much room for dating? It meant she got to find guys like Carter.

"Home sweet home," she announced, turning on the lights.

Carter looked around. There was the kitchenette and the door to the bathroom, both to the right of the front door. The bed was on the wall to the left of the door, and then the rest of it—all the rest of it —was art.

"Is your bedspread *Starry Night*?" Carter asked.

Leticia nodded, bouncing back onto it. "You like Van Gogh?"

"I like art," Carter replied, closing the front door behind him. He shucked off his shirt and Leticia licked her lips. Yes, she was greatly appreciating being able to ogle Carter in proper lighting.

Carter suddenly huffed out a laugh, running his fingers through his hair. "What?" Leticia asked. He just shook his head. "What?" She asked again.

He sighed. "You're about to think I'm the cheesiest ever."

She nudged him with her foot. "You gave me two orgasms. I'll give you a free pass."

He climbed onto the bed so that he was hovering over her again. "I was going to say that I like art, like you."

Leticia groaned. "As in, I'm a work of art? That is cheesy."

"Hey, you said I got a free pass!"

"That I did." She poked at him. "So, just what can all these muscles do, huh?"

"Are you asking me to show off for you?"

"A little."

Carter gave her a wicked grin. "Take off your dress."

Leticia shivered at his tone of voice and quickly took off her dress. Carter pulled off his pants and she could see that he was hard again—but not quite hard enough.

Before Carter could continue with whatever he had planned, Leticia slid to her knees and took him into her mouth. Carter made an honest-to-God choking noise, his hands flying to her hair to steady himself.

"Jesus Christ," he stuttered.

Leticia swirled her tongue around the head and then pulled back. "Nope, just me."

Carter laughed a little but then she slowly started feeding him back into her mouth and his laugh turned into a groan. Leticia had to work hard not to smile as she started working more and more of him into her mouth. She loved doing this, loved the musky, heady taste of him in her mouth and the weight of him on her tongue as he stretched her lips wide around him. He was thick enough that she didn't think she'd be able to deep throat him, not without practice, but Carter certainly didn't seem to be complaining. He cursed loudly and repeatedly, and she could feel his legs shaking as he tried to keep himself from thrusting into her mouth.

She took him down again and again, sliding her tongue up the underside and then tonguing the slit before bobbing back down. She could have done this for ages, but she could feel precum bursting over her tongue repeatedly and she knew that Carter was close—and she didn't want it to end like this. She wanted to know what he'd had planned.

She pulled off and looked up at him through her lashes. "I think you said something about showing off for me?"

Carter growled, and then she was being hauled up into his arms. She gave a little scream and dug her nails into his shoulders as—Jesus Christ—he lifted her up and slammed her against the wall. Leticia wrapped her legs around him, feeling him pin her there by the hips. Fuck, he didn't even need to use his hands. His legs and his body weight were holding her up all on their own.

"Oh my God," she choked out. This was strong, this was unbelievably strong. This was going-to-touch-myself-to-this-for-ages levels of strong.

Carter gave her a mischievous grin. "You ready?"

Leticia nodded. She should still be pretty loose and ready from the last round. Sure enough, Carter slid in easily, just enough resistance there to give it that pleasant burn. He braced his hands on either side of her head and Leticia held on with both her arms and her legs.

For a moment they just breathed together. Their foreheads were touching and it was like they were in this tiny cocoon of space, just the two of them.

Then Carter started to move.

He was rough and fast, just like before, and Leticia couldn't keep quiet. She silently apologized to any neighbors that might hear her because she couldn't stop crying out. He was hitting that perfect spot inside of her and just the fact that he was holding her up like this, that he was strong enough to fuck her like an animal while *holding her up against a wall*—she was coming embarrassingly quickly, sobbing out Carter's name.

He kept fucking her through it, until she went from orgasm to over sensitized, and then he was kissing her and thumbing at that spot just below her ear that made her melt and she was coming all over again, or having a second wave, or something, screaming into his mouth.

They collapsed on the bed, Carter half on top of her. Leticia's chest was heaving and she had spots dancing in front of her eyes.

"I think my legs are numb," Carter admitted.

"Sex against the wall was your idea," she replied, laughing tiredly. "Would you like some water?"

"That'd be great."

Stumbling to her feet, she walked on unsteady legs to the kitchenette. The one good thing about her tiny apartment: it didn't take a lot of walking to get where you needed to go. And there was always a wall conveniently handy to lean on.

After they drank some water, Leticia was ready to tumble into bed. She needed a shower but she could do that in the morning before picking up the cake for the twins' birthday party.

Carter, however, looked like he was getting ready to go.

"Do you want to use the shower or anything?" Leticia asked. She ignored the odd twinge in her stomach at the idea of Carter not spending the night. She hadn't had a guy spend the night at her place in years. But waking up early for some lazy morning sex had seemed fun.

She mentally shook herself. This was a one-night stand. She did this kind of thing all the time. No reason to get sentimental. Carter obviously had places to be and she wasn't going to get upset about it.

"I'm okay, I can shower at home." Carter pulled his clothes back on. He pulled out his phone and Leticia saw him fire up Uber. "Sorry about just skipping out on you. I just have to be up early tomorrow."

"No problem, I understand. Gotta check on your friends, too."

Carter laughed. "Oh man, that too. I trust the groom will have found his way home okay. The others... I should probably double-check on them."

"No problem."

Carter finished doing up his belt and walked over to her. He placed his hands lightly on her elbows and gave her a soft kiss. "This was really fun. Thank you."

"Of course." Leticia found herself wrong-footed. Carter was being very sweet, and she had no idea how to react to it. "Anytime," she added, going for flirtatious.

Carter winked at her and then opened the front door. "Have a good night!"

"You, too!"

Leticia stared at the closed door after he left. Was it really that odd to her that someone would thank her for sex? Surely other guys had thanked her.

Except... they hadn't. She'd get off with them, at the club or at their apartment or whatever (or an alley, which when Sharon had found out had nearly given her a heart attack), and then she'd beat a hasty retreat and the men had always seemed fine with it. Now the man was the one retreating, since it was her place, and he was being more gracious about it than she'd ever been when she was slipping out the door.

Leticia shook herself, this time physically, and decided she'd take a shower that night after all. It would help ease any aches out of her muscles from that last round.

Maybe it was time to stop the one-night stands, she thought. She still didn't think she had time for a proper relationship but she wasn't getting any younger and if a guy behaving a little differently was throwing her off, it might be time to call it quits. Focus just on her job, and find a way to make more room in her schedule for when the right person came along. She'd just gotten this promotion, after all. That meant more responsibilities. And she had to train whoever they brought in to replace her. Focusing on her job would be just what she needed.

Leticia tumbled into bed and set her alarm so she'd wake up in time. Melanie might forgive her for forgetting to grab the cake but Tom wouldn't, and Sharon especially wouldn't.

She drifted off to sleep, trying not to think too much about Carter.

CHAPTER 2

*C*arter looked at himself in the mirror. "What the hell," he said out loud.

He didn't do one-night stands. Not even before Olivia. He'd met her in his Introduction to Architecture seminar, for crying out loud.

What had he been thinking?

Well, he knew what he'd been thinking. That is, he hadn't been thinking at all. He'd been entranced by a gorgeous woman with curves and a great ass and a gleam in her eye and he'd let his dick do the decision making.

Not that Leticia had been awful or anything. She'd been amazing, in fact. If he closed his eyes, he could still remember how she tasted on his tongue, the way she'd rode his lap, the desperate screams she'd made as he'd fucked her against the wall. The way she'd looked up at him after sucking his dick...

Carter quickly focused on brushing his teeth. Nope, he was not going to dwell on any of that. He had to hurry and pick up Molly from his parents.

When he'd told Mom and Dad he needed them to watch Molly for the night, he'd told them that it was because of the party and he'd be out late taking care of whatever stupid decisions Brian and the others

19

made. He hadn't thought that he'd be the one making questionable decisions.

But what was questionable about it?

He'd used protection. He hadn't been drunk. He'd gotten home safely so he could wake up in time to pick up Molly. He'd checked in on Brian and the others and all of them were fine.

Maybe it was just the residual guilt. Olivia had passed away a few years ago, but she still lingered in the back of his mind at times. He was so used to the idea of her presence there that he often forgot about it until moments like these.

He didn't have a reason to be guilty, he reminded himself. Olivia would have wanted him to move on, and it had been years. Molly needed another adult presence in her life. She needed a woman, someone besides her grandmother, to help her. God knew that half the time Carter had no idea what to say to her.

Perhaps the fact that he'd had a one-night stand proved that he was ready to date again. Of course there was a world of difference between getting laid and investing in someone emotionally, but still... It had to be a sign.

He finished getting ready and hopped in the car to pick up Molly. Mom and Dad never complained about babysitting her but he didn't want to take advantage of them. Dad, especially, appreciated it. He was the one feeling his age, more than Mom, and Molly was their only grandchild. But that wasn't an excuse to abandon Molly with them for however long he felt like it. He'd said he'd pick Molly up at ten and he'd meant it.

Of course, at the time, he hadn't thought that he'd be working off of so little sleep. Thank God he hadn't stayed the night at Leticia's. As much as he'd have liked to, it wouldn't have been wise. Her apartment was clear across town from his, and his parents' house was an additional twenty minutes away from that, in the suburbs.

The idea of morning sex had appealed to him. He could imagine what Leticia would look like, sleepy-eyed, all that golden skin laid out just for him. He could have woken her up with teasing kisses, stroking lightly at her sides, making her fall apart slowly.

Ah, well. At least he had the night to remember, and what a night it had been.

When he arrived at Mom and Dad's, he found Molly ready to go and sitting on the front step. She was more independent at times than he'd like. He was continually worried that she'd run away to live in the New York Met museum or something like that book. But she was also always so happy to see him. It made his heart clench.

If he was going to start dating, then he would have to be careful. Molly deserved to have women in her life that were the best. He wasn't going to bring home someone who wouldn't care about Molly and see how special she was.

"Dad!" Molly yelled. She stood up and waved as he pulled into the driveway.

"Hey there, Artemisia," Carter said, getting out of the car.

It was his special nickname for her. Artemisia Gentileschi was one of his favorite artists and had been a gifted painter, her first major piece being completed when she was only seventeen years old. Artemisia's father had also been a painter and involved in the art world, just like Carter was. Molly had always had a huge talent and love for art, and so the nickname had come about.

Carter had never told Molly this, but another part of why he called her that was that Gentileschi had lost her mother at a young age, just like Molly had. Gentileschi's father had never given her a good replacement figure, and Gentileschi's work had shown that craving for a strong female relationship and the importance of female solidarity. It was a reminder to Carter—he didn't just want a wife. Molly needed a mother.

Molly ran up and hugged him, and he hugged her back just as tightly. "Did you have fun with Nan and Pops?" He asked. Carter smiled at the thought of Molly's names for her grandparents. Since Molly had assigned them these names a few years ago, Carter himself had stopped thinking of them as Mom and Dad, and referred to them only by their duly appointed grandparent names.

She nodded. "They're cleaning up breakfast and said I could wait for you. Do you want some pancakes?"

"Sure, why not?"

His parents greeted him with warmth and he helped himself to the leftover pancakes. Once Molly was occupied with finishing a drawing, he drew his parents into the kitchen so she couldn't overhear. There he put forth the idea of dating.

"Do you think it's time?" He asked. "Molly's only seven."

"I've found that children are more adaptable than we think they are," Nan pointed out.

"But what if I date someone and bring them into Molly's life and then they leave?" Carter asked. "I don't want to hurt her. And, I mean —dying, that—nothing is like that. But Olivia didn't choose to go. She didn't want to leave us. And Molly knows that. But if a girlfriend walks out on me, that's different. She's choosing to leave us. I don't want Molly to feel abandoned that way."

"Then don't tell Molly at first," Pops suggested. "Go on a few dates and make sure this woman is serious before you do anything."

"Even if your relationship ends," Nan added gently, "Doesn't mean that she'll walk away from Molly. A girl can have multiple mother-figures in her life."

"And you need to think about yourself, too," Pops said. "Now, you know we don't like to pry, but it's been four years. Molly is your main concern and that's how it should be, but you need someone, too."

Carter thought about it. He'd really wanted to spend the night with Leticia. He must have been lonelier than he'd realized.

"All right," he said. "It'll give you guys an excuse to babysit her more, if nothing else."

Nan laughed. "That was our nefarious plan all along."

Carter tried to ignore the nervous twinge in his gut. He could do this. He could date again.

CHAPTER 3

*W*hoever had invented Monday mornings should be put in the stocks.

Leticia was aware that people did not in fact use stocks anymore, but she thought they should revive the tradition. Just for whoever thought Monday mornings were a great idea.

Saturday had been great. She'd woken up refreshed, if suffering from a pleasant ache in her legs. She'd picked up the cake and then driven to Jonas's apartment. Debbie's apartment was always a mess, Sharon had protested that she always hosted everything, and the twins weren't about to host their own party, so Jonas had taken up the mantel.

It had been fun, as always. Jonas had tons of hilarious stories to share. They'd all taken turns giving a toast to Melanie and Tom. Debbie and Mel were much easier to be around now that they'd finally gotten over themselves and started dating. Sharon and Ross had been sickeningly cute, and Leticia had gotten to put her hand to Sharon's growing stomach and feel the baby kick. Sharon was being stubborn and not letting the doctor tell her whether it was going to be a boy or a girl. Leticia knew that Ross was hoping for a girl, but she didn't care. She was going to spoil the baby either way.

She was a little nervous about the whole baby thing, actually. She'd never been comfortable around kids. Not that she disliked them. She just didn't know what to do with them. It had made for a few awkward situations, growing up with tons of cousins that she visited every Christmas in Mexico, all of her aunts and uncles were confused when she didn't want to hold a baby or play babysitter.

Leticia knew she could be a bit much. She was brash and blunt and loud. How was she supposed to reconcile that with a child, something that needed a gentle touch and extra guidance, someone who wouldn't get her sarcasm or her dirty jokes?

And—if she was really being honest—she'd never thought of babies as that cute. Maybe one day when she was married she'd adopt an older kid, but babies? No way. They weren't repulsive or anything, she just didn't get why everybody made such a fuss over them.

But for the sake of her best friend, she'd find a way. Any child of Sharon's was automatically a part of Leticia's heart. She was sure that, when the time came, she'd find a way to get over whatever hang ups she had and be the best not-blood-related aunt in the world.

Sunday had been a wonderfully lazy day right up until Jonas had texted her, asking her to take him out to dance. She hadn't planned on going out again after Friday night but, hey, she wasn't about to say no. They hit up a gay club, which Leticia honestly hadn't minded. Normally she'd needle Jonas about taking her somewhere he could get laid and she couldn't, but she'd found herself oddly unwilling to find someone to sleep with.

To say that she couldn't get Carter out of her head was a bit melo-dramatic. She just didn't feel like sleeping with anyone else, that was all. The fact that this had never happened before wasn't anything to worry about. It was just a sign that she needed to focus on work, like she'd thought.

Then she'd stayed out too late—or really, too early—and now Monday morning was here and she kind of wanted to find a way to kill the sun.

"Why does it have to be so bright out," she grumbled.

"I take it that's code for an extra shot of espresso?" The barista asked. Her name was Hal and she'd been making coffee for Leticia for the past year now, every morning when Leticia stopped by the place on her way to the museum. Hal was pretty good at reading Leticia's moods by now.

"Yes, please," Leticia groaned. She'd need all the caffeine that she could get.

"Coming right up!" Hal winked at her. "Oh, you wouldn't believe the guy that came in twenty minutes ago. Blonde, built—I totally wanted to give him my number but I think he was like ten years older than I am and, also, I chickened out."

"You'll never get a date if you don't take a risk," Leticia pointed out, thinking of her own blonde and built date from Friday night. She shivered pleasantly at the memory. "And shouldn't you be focusing on that senior thesis paper?"

"Shouldn't you be at work already?" Hal shot back, handing Leticia her coffee.

"Touché, kid."

Caffeine now happily working its way through her system, Leticia walked around the corner to the museum. She did love her job. Deciding what art the public got to see, arranging it so that it flowed throughout the entire building, telling a story... she'd never had much talent for making art herself, but she loved caring for it and sharing it with the world.

When she walked in, she was greeted by cheerful "good mornings" from the security desk. She scowled at them. The audacity of being this chipper this early in the morning.

She made her way to her office, set down her coffee, and proceeded to groan at the stack of paperwork already on her desk. Really? When they'd said she'd get the job of head curator, all she'd been able to think about was the creative side of things. She hadn't considered just how much goddamn paperwork she'd have to do.

Hopefully, when they hired her replacement, she could foist some of that paperwork off onto them.

There was a knock at her door. Leticia straightened up and double-checked her hair. Did she have circles under her eyes? Was it obvious that she'd been covered in glitter and dancing with just her bra on the night before?

What? It was a gay bar and all the guys had been shirtless. Also, she might have been drunk.

Leticia opened the door to find none other than her boss standing there: the museum director.

"Mr. Horowitz!" Leticia put on her best smile. "What can I do for you?"

"I've told you, Leticia, it's just David, please." Mr. Horowitz smiled. He seemed relaxed, happy even, which was rare. Usually he looked like he'd just heard the Louvre had burned down or something equally awful. "I know you're probably hard at work, but I wanted to introduce you to your replacement for assistant curator."

"Thank God," Leticia blurted out. "No offense, sir, but doing the paperwork of two jobs has been a little exhausting."

"Of course, and this man comes highly recommended. He worked in several museums up in New York City until four years ago. Since then, he was in charge of the Children's Museum, but we managed to poach him from them."

"I'm sure you offered him quite a substantial raise to manage that?" Leticia asked.

"We did what we had to do. The Children's Museum has far too many employees already, and we desperately needed someone with experience in order to fill your shoes."

"I'm flattered," Leticia said, and she honestly meant it. She'd always liked to think that her work as assistant curator hadn't gone unnoticed. Her former boss and predecessor as Head Curator, Laura Weiss, had retired only a month or so ago, but she'd been giving Leticia a ton of responsibility long before then.

"Now, his background is with Botticelli and the Italian masters…"

"Oh Lord, don't tell me he's a snob."

Mr. Horowitz laughed. "But I can assure you, he's excited to work with contemporary art. I was thinking that he would help you to show visitors how contemporary art is in conversation with the art that came before it."

"Sounds good."

Mr. Horowitz started walking and Leticia hurried to follow him. He led her past her old office, where presumably the new hire would work, and instead took her to the Scaife galleries. "I left him in here to wander around," Mr. Horowitz explained. "Give him a feel for things before I thrust him into an office."

"This is why I actually don't hate you," Leticia quipped. "I know it's tradition to hate one's boss but you're not half bad."

"Thank you," Mr. Horowitz said dryly. "Pleasing you is my one joy in life."

Leticia laughed at his sarcasm, throwing her head back, so she literally ran into someone as she turned the corner. She stepped back, disoriented, and then had to clench down on her jaw to keep her mouth from dropping open.

It was Carter.

"Ah, Mr. Bolton!" Mr. Horowitz beamed. He was obviously oblivious to the crisis that Leticia was having inside. "This is your new boss, our Head Curator, Leticia Perra. Leticia, this is Carter Bolton, the new hire for assistant curator."

Carter stared at her, and Leticia stared back. For a moment it felt like she was frozen. How could this be possible? Had Hal put some kind of hallucinogen in her coffee? Was she actually still asleep and having a nightmare?

Then she realized that Mr. Horowitz was staring and if she didn't start acting normal in the next two seconds, she was going to have a lot of explaining to do. "Mr. Bolton," she said, glad to hear that her voice was even. She held out her hand for him to shake.

"Ms. Perra," Carter replied, shaking her hand. His hand was large, his grip firm, and she couldn't help but remember where he'd had those hands on her Friday night. They'd been on her hips, spanning her back, tangled in her hair while she'd taken his dick in her mouth...

Leticia dropped his hand like it had scalded her. Shit, shit, shit. How the hell was she supposed to handle this?

Mr. Horowitz cleared his throat and Leticia realized that she'd been staring at Carter in silence. She was so screwed. "I'll let you two get acquainted," her boss said, and then he was walking out of the gallery.

She was alone with her one-night stand. The one-night stand that had blown her mind.

She was in so much trouble.

CHAPTER 4

*C*arter was screwed.

Leticia, the smoking hot one-night stand from Friday, his first one-night stand in… well, ever, was apparently his boss.

Well, damn.

She was as beautiful as he'd remembered, perhaps even more so now that he could see her properly put together and in the light of day. Her thick hair that he'd loved gripping Friday night was now curled into thick ringlets that fell down her back. She was wearing only light makeup, enough to highlight her dark, warm eyes. Instead of a skimpy, clingy dress, she was wearing a plaid vintage dress with dark leggings and wedge booties. It made her look adorable and sexy all at the same time.

But now, he wanted to shove her against a wall all over again. Peel those layers off of her. Tug on that hair. See if he could smudge her makeup and suck some bruises into her creamy skin.

Carter straightened his shoulders. No. He was not going to do that. He was going to be professional. A one-night stand didn't mean that Leticia was still attracted to him in any way or that she still wanted to sleep with him. And a relationship with his boss… well, even if Molly wasn't a factor to consider, a workplace romance was probably a bad idea on several levels. What if he fucking screwed it up? This job paid well and got him unfettered access to the beautiful art that he loved. Nothing against his former job, of course—he'd loved opening kids' minds to art—but this was where his heart really was. He didn't want to jeopardize that. And God forbid he misstep and get hauled in for workplace harassment.

"Mr. Horowitz told me a bit about what this job would entail when he interviewed me," he said, "And I'm sure he showed you my resume, but I was hoping you could take some time and tell me about what you'll expect from me?"

Leticia took a deep breath. Perhaps she, too, was trying to tamp down on any kind of attraction. It was both dangerous and comforting to think that she might still be just as attracted to him as he was to her. "Right. Yes. Follow me?"

It's good to see you again, Carter wanted to say. He kept his mouth shut instead and nodded as Leticia indicated that they start walking.

Leticia started talking about the art and how she had it all laid out, and what art they weren't allowed to move, and how they chose the temporary exhibits for the contemporary art. Carter found it hard to concentrate.

What were the odds that the woman he'd randomly met at a club, the one he'd had sex with... out of the entirety of Pittsburgh, was his boss? What were the chances of that? Was it some kind of sign? Or was the universe just laughing at him especially hard right now?

It was almost like somebody was mocking him for deciding to try dating again.

Unless this was a sign that Leticia was the person that he was supposed to be dating.

Nope, nope, way too many ways that could blow up in his face.

Leticia kept talking, but he could hear the determined undertone in her voice and suspected that she was working just as hard to keep things professional as he was. Finally, she stopped and let out a huff of frustration.

"Everything okay?" He asked.

"The guy I slept with on Friday is now my assistant," Leticia said. "How would you feel?"

"I'm not sure. How would you feel if the woman you slept with on Friday was now your boss?"

Leticia laughed. Carter could feel a band of tension around his chest loosen up a little bit.

"Look, I have no idea what to do with this, either," he admitted. "Maybe… we can just try and keep things professional? I'm sure we're not the first two people who've ever dealt with something like this."

Leticia nodded, sobering up. Her forehead puckered in a way that was kind of adorable. "I agree. I really love this job, and I'm sure you want to keep yours. I'd hate for things to get awkward."

"I'm glad to hear it." Carter breathed out a slow sigh of relief. "So, tell me about the museum."

Leticia seemed equal parts relieved and excited, smiling up at the artwork around them. "My pleasure."

Her face lit up as she talked, her passion clear in the way her hands flew around animatedly, a smile flickering constantly at the corners of her mouth. He'd known that whoever his new boss would be, they had to know a lot about art. He was glad to see that Leticia was passionate about it as well.

She was even more beautiful than that night, he thought, now that he was able to observe her in the light of day. She looked just as much in her element here in the museum as she had in the club. Confidence oozed from every one of her pores.

Dammit. When he'd decided that it might be time to start dating again, he hadn't meant that as permission to keep being attracted to his coworker. No, not just his coworker—his boss. He really wanted this job and he couldn't let anything jeopardize it. He was just going to have to find a way to deal with it.

It had to go away eventually, right?

CHAPTER 5

*L*eticia rolled her eyes at Sharon. "I didn't get up to anything, no."

Sharon finished pouring the wine for everyone—minus herself, given her condition—and set the bottle down. "Oh, sorry. Allow me to rephrase that. Did you get up to any*one* last weekend?"

"You had that look," Jonas said, helping himself to the box of crackers on the counter. Sharon had long given up on plating everything nicely and tended to just pile food up on her kitchen island for everyone to rifle through.

Leticia folded her arms. "What look?"

"The..." Jonas waved his hand vaguely in the air. "The glowing post-sex look. The one Sharon has on her face all the time."

"I suppose you expect me to be offended by that," Ross said, walking up to grab his glass of wine. "How dare we be happily married with an active sex life, and all that."

"Point is," Sharon said, loudly, "Who was he?"

"There wasn't anyone!" Leticia replied. She wasn't sure why she was protesting so much. Normally she would have been happy to share the details about her one-night stand with Carter. She did it all the time with her other hook ups. But this was different. Carter was her coworker. It embarrassed her that she'd made the mistake of sleeping with him, even though she'd had no way of knowing at the time who he was.

Actually, she might have, if she'd taken the time to talk to him before she'd slept with him. She would have found out where he worked, what he did, and he would probably have told her about his new job. It wasn't like he was required to keep it a secret or anything. Then this whole embarrassing scene this morning could have been avoided.

Leticia picked up her own glass of wine and took a sip, contemplating. Maybe this was a sign that she needed to think about dating more seriously? Maybe the universe was having her latest hook up come back to bite her in the ass as a sign to get a move on. Once Carter was properly trained, she'd hopefully have more time for things like proper dates. Perhaps she should start considering that.

"Hello? Earth to Letty," Sharon said, snapping her fingers. "C'mon, you think I don't know when you're hiding something?"

"Maybe it was something embarrassing?" Debbie called from the couch, where she was sitting with her head tucked into the curve of Melanie's shoulder.

"It wasn't—" Leticia started, only to realize that saying 'it wasn't embarrassing' would mean admitting that 'it' had happened.

Debbie caught onto that. "Ha!" She crowed triumphantly.

"Damn lawyers," Leticia muttered.

"So?" Jonas asked. "What happened? Who was he?"

"Who was who?" Tom asked, emerging from the bathroom. "Oh, wait, did Leticia find another guy?"

"He—" Leticia sighed, giving up. Her friends were only going to keep poking at her until she gave in. "Okay, yes, last Friday night I met this guy at one of the clubs. He was great, we had sex twice, I took him back to my place, etc. I had a great weekend with you guys, and then I went into work on Monday."

"And?" Sharon probed, knowing there was more to the story. Ross chuckled, privately amused by her, and pressed an absentminded kiss to her temple.

Leticia took a deep breath. "You know how I just got promoted to head curator, right?"

"What does this have to do with the guy?" She heard Melanie whisper to Debbie, who shushed her.

"Right," Sharon said, nodding.

"So they need someone to fill my former role as assistant curator," Leticia explained. "So, I walked in on Monday morning, and found…"

"Oh my God," Ross said, jumping to the truth. "Your Friday night guy is now your assistant."

"What?" Jonas yelped.

Leticia didn't answer just yet, but she was sure the heat she could feel creeping up her face spoke volumes.

Ross shrugged. "What can I say, I know a little something about weird coincidences."

Sharon laughed. Leticia had to smile at that, remembering the coincidences surrounding how Sharon and Ross had gotten together. That night when Sharon had gotten into the car crash had been one of the worst of Leticia's life. She'd been on the phone with her best friend, helpless, hearing the car swerve and metal bend and break, hearing Sharon scream in pain—and then hearing nothing as Sharon passed out, forcing Leticia to call an ambulance and then jump into her car and race to the nearest hospital.

Thank God Ross had operated on her, and thank God it had only been her leg. Leticia was grateful, in a way, that it had happened because it had led to Sharon and Ross falling in love and getting married. But she hoped to never, ever have to endure something like that night again, gripped with fear and unable to help.

"Is he your new assistant?" Melanie asked, twisting around from her position on the couch to look Leticia in the eye.

Leticia nodded. "I mean, he's not my direct assistant. He doesn't fetch me coffee or make appointments or anything. But he's my right-hand man when it comes to running the museum. He's the second in command."

"So you're his boss," Tom mused. He chuckled. "Man, Letty, you do sure know how to pick 'em."

"I didn't know who he was!" Leticia protested. "How was I supposed to know who he was, huh?"

"She's got a point," Sharon said. "I mean, what are the odds?"

Everyone looked pointedly at Sharon and Ross.

Sharon laughed. "All right, sorry. But seriously, Leticia, you had no idea of knowing. I'm sure he's just as embarrassed as you are."

"Even more so, maybe," Jonas said. "After all, you're the one who's in charge. You could fire him if you wanted."

"I wouldn't fire him over something that neither of us had any control over or knowledge of," Leticia replied. "That would just be unfair."

"How are you going to keep working with him?" Debbie asked.

Leticia shrugged. "I don't know. I mean, people have one-night stands all the time. It doesn't mean anything, or at least it doesn't have to mean anything if we don't want it to."

"Only Letty would end up in this situation," Tom said, shaking his head in amusement.

"That's because you're boring and never go out anywhere anymore," Leticia shot back.

"Stuck with a hot coworker," Sharon teased, clucking her tongue. "However will you survive?"

"True," Melanie said. "Just because you can't order off the menu doesn't mean you can't at least look at it."

Leticia laughed. "Honestly, I'm sure this is something that'll just blow over and we'll laugh about it in a few weeks. It'll be a funny story to tell people at parties. I'm not worried."

The others all smiled and moved on. Debbie asked Melanie something about work, Tom and Ross continued a long-standing argument about football, and Jonas went to go pick a movie from the DVD collection.

Only Sharon seemed to see that Leticia was still nervous—and that she'd been lying when she said she wasn't worried. Sharon laid her hand over Leticia's, smiling gently.

"It'll work out," she told her. "Whatever way it's supposed to work out, it will. Whatever you're worried about, I'm sure it won't be as bad as all that."

Leticia let out a shaky breath. "I suppose. I just—the museum is my home. That art, it's my life. It means the world to me. I hate the idea that a place that's so special to me might become somewhere I don't like going to because of a coworker."

"I highly doubt it will be," Sharon replied. "C'mon, when I was so worried about this whole thing with Ross and freaking out, weren't you the one who told me to calm down? And you were right, it all worked out for the best."

Leticia nodded. It was true. Sharon and Ross were still deeply in love, had a beautiful house, and were expecting their first child. It didn't get more picture-perfect than that.

"If I can manage to come out on top when you and I both know I'm a huge mess just waiting to happen," Sharon teased, "Then I know that you'll be okay too. This doesn't have to ruin anything."

Leticia turned her hand over so that she could intertwine her fingers with Sharon's and give her hand a squeeze. "Thanks, hon. I appreciate it."

"Of course. What are best friends for, huh?" Sharon winked at her.

"Sharon?" Jonas called. "Care to explain why you're missing the third film in the Dark Knight Trilogy?"

"Ask Ross," Sharon replied.

"Throwing me under the bus," Ross mourned. "I knew this day would come."

"You brought this fate upon yourself, dear," Sharon replied, winking at him.

As good-natured bickering started up among the group, Leticia relaxed back against the island. Sharon was right, she thought. She was going to be okay. It was a hiccup, and it was a little embarrassing, but she was going to be fine. No reason to freak out.

Even in her own mind the argument sounded weak.

CHAPTER 6

*N*ormally, Monday was the only day of the week that Leticia dreaded. She and Monday would be locked in perpetual battle until the day she died. But now it was Tuesday morning and she was dreading work all the same.

Yesterday had been her first day working with Carter and it had mostly consisted of showing him the ropes. He'd seemed perfectly professional and happy to learn from her, but she didn't know what the next day would bring. The teasing from her friends last night had helped a little, actually. It had shown her how ridiculous this whole situation was.

Leticia figured she could treat this like a huge deal and freak out, or she could treat it as something amusing and lighthearted and not make it into anything she didn't want it to be. She decided on the latter.

It seemed that Carter had decided the same thing, because when he met her at their offices this morning, he had a professional but genuine smile on his face.

That was another thing—their offices were right next to each other. As if Leticia wouldn't have been seeing him enough as it was.

"Morning," Carter said. His smile widened as Leticia sent him a death glare. "Ah, not a morning person, I see."

"Whatever gave you that impression?" Leticia replied, clutching her coffee for dear life. So she wasn't her best in the morning. Sue her.

Carter laughed. "So, what would you like me to do today?"

Leticia thought about that. "I still have my planner and things from when I had your job. I can give it to you to read, it'll help you get a good idea of what you'll be expected to do every day here. If you tell me what you did at your previous job, I can let you take on the responsibilities that are similar, and I can start to coach you through anything that's different. Like our filing system." She pulled a face, and Carter laughed again.

"Sure. Want to grab lunch to go over everything?' He shrugged. "You guys are easing me into this, which is really nice, but I feel kind of bad. I know you're doing a lot of my work on top of your own right now."

"I'm almost used to it at this point," Leticia replied. "I've been doing it for a few months now. A few more days isn't going to kill me. I remember when I first got here, they threw me right in, I felt like I was drowning."

"All right then, if you're sure. Noon work for you?"

"Works great."

Carter opened her office door for her, seeing as her arms were full with her coffee and paperwork. "Thanks."

Leticia closed the door behind her and set her paperwork down. Dammit. He was as attractive as she'd remembered. And here she'd spent all of last night telling herself that he wasn't that attractive, that obviously she had exaggerated in her head.

Nope. He looked like goddamn Captain America.

Just her luck.

Her morning flew by quickly. She sent her old notes and paper-work and things over to Carter so that he could get a look at them. She didn't want to baby him, but she could still vividly remember how much she'd panicked those first few weeks. She'd thought that she was prepared for the job and she had been, but there was a difference between being prepared and actually experiencing it. Responsibility was responsibility, but getting used to the particular quirks and systems and customs of a new place took time. She wanted Carter to experience as much of it in a positive way as possible.

The rest of the morning was spent in handling paperwork, making some calls, and dealing with a couple of agents and representatives for artists. Artists were split about halfway down the middle on common sense. Fifty percent of them were reasonable human beings, like Tom. The other half were exactly how every single stereotype made them sound. Except worse.

The problem, Leticia had found, was that agents and others who represented artists had to work in the best interests of their client. This meant that half the time the agents acted as though their client was God's gift to both art museums and humanity in general.

It could make them pretty insufferable.

By the time lunch rolled around, Leticia had completely lost track of the time. A soft knock on her door startled her—she was in the middle of drafting an email.

"Hey, you still free?" Carter asked. Leticia tried very hard not to stare at the light blue button-up shirt he was wearing, the top couple of buttons undone. It really wasn't fair that he was this attractive—or that she knew how he looked with all of those clothes off.

"Yeah, sorry." She quickly saved the email draft. She'd get back to it later with fresh eyes. "Just trying to find a way to say 'fuck you' without actually saying that."

Carter laughed. "I understand that. We get a lot of donors back at the children's museum. People are almost always willing to donate to something for kids, y'know? But then they think their money means they can run the place. It's pretty exhausting."

Leticia let him hold the door for her as she exited. "There's this great place just down the street. If you like Thai food?"

"Sure, Thai sounds great."

She'd gone to this place plenty of times over the years. It was right by the coffee shop, which was how she'd found out about it. Ordering her food and then sprinkling as many chili flakes on it as she could until her lips were tingling was sometimes the best part of her day. It was a real mom and pop place, run by a couple that had emigrated back when they were in their twenties and were now in their sixties but still ran the kitchen. Leticia loved them.

Once they were seated, Leticia continued their conversation. "We get that sometimes with donors as well. If anyone gives you a hard time just redirect them to me. I've got no problem being the one that takes the heat."

"Yeah, you strike me as someone who doesn't take bullshit," Carter noted.

Mrs. Bunnag, the woman who owned the place with her husband, came up to them with some menus. "Leticia! Back again. And with this handsome gentleman?"

"Mrs. Bunnag, this is my new coworker, Carter," Leticia said, introducing them. "I got that promotion and he has my old job now."

"She's my boss," Carter explained, smiling.

"Ah, so you two will be working together a lot, yes?" Mrs. Bunnag said. Leticia nearly groaned and face-planted onto the table. She should have known that she wouldn't be able to escape some match-making. For years now, the Bunnags had been asking her when she was going to find a 'nice young man.'

"He's just a coworker," Leticia told her firmly. "And can I have my usual?"

"Just a coworker, of course," Mrs. Bunnag replied, in a tone that said she didn't believe Leticia in the slightest. "And for you?"

"I'll take the number four?" Carter asked.

Leticia nodded. "Good choice."

She waited until Mrs. Bunnag went away before leaning in. "That's a good one to get if you're not used to spice."

Carter raised an eyebrow. "Who says I'm not used to spice?"

"Says the Latina to the white boy. You guys think salt and pepper are the only spices that exist."

Carter laughed. "All right, fair point." He gestured subtly towards where Mrs. Bunnag had disappeared. "Am I right in thinking she's tried to set you up before?"

"You have no idea." Leticia rolled her eyes. "Every day I come in here it feels like she knows someone I should let her set me up with."

"I get that. My parents think it's high time I started dating again."

Leticia frowned. "Bad breakup?" She knew all about those. Not that she'd ever had one herself. A bad breakup usually required you to have been in a serious relationship in the first place. But she'd held Sharon's and Debbie's and Tom's and Jonas's hands all through the heartbreak before.

Carter shook his head. "Um, something like that."

Leticia could tell he was holding something back but, well, who was she to judge? He'd just met her and she didn't know what kind of crap might have happened to him in his last relationship. Jonas still didn't really like to talk about his last boyfriend because of how awful the experience was.

"Well, I wish I could empathize," she said, "But I've never been anywhere close to a serious relationship so..."

"Oh come on, no serious boyfriends ever?" Carter asked. "That can't be possible."

He seemed genuinely interested, but Leticia suspected the slight change of subject was also to draw them away from such a delicate topic. She decided to go along with it. It wasn't her place to get him to spill all his secrets. "I just never found anyone I wanted to be serious with. Didn't help that I think I've got a bit of a vibe about me."

"A vibe?" Carter chuckled.

"Shut up, I'm serious! Like... You know those people—you meet them and you've got no proof, but you just know they're an asshole. I think I've got the same thing but like, as a bad girl. People want to sleep with me but they don't want to properly date me, y'know? And I never had anyone that I was into enough to try and fight against it when they just wanted a simple hookup."

"Fair enough," Carter said. "I think that's pretty unfair, though. To just make that kind of assumption about you."

"Well, I mean, I go out to clubs every weekend and I'm not known for my loose-fitting clothes. I can see why they make that assumption."

"You could be going out to clubs just to dance," Carter pointed out. "And just because you want to show off what you've got doesn't mean you want people to touch it. It's still an assumption."

Leticia was caught off-guard by his sweetness. "Thank you."

"Of course." Carter smiled at her, and Leticia melted just a little. "And you look perfectly professional to me."

Leticia looked down at her blouse and slacks. "Ah, well, that's because I'm at work. I'm a very serious head curator for a very serious museum, didn't you know? I have to look the part."

"Oh yes." Carter nodded. "How else are you going to get those artists to listen to you?"

"Ugh, don't even get me started." Leticia smiled up at Mrs. Bunnag as their food was delivered. "Everyone talks about the tortured artist, lack of self-esteem, that sort of thing, but I think they took that and turned it into a need to act like they're the most important person in the room." Leticia sighed. "But, frankly, I'll take them over the board."

"Ah, civilians with opinions." Carter rolled his eyes. "God save us."

"How are we supposed to get people from every walk of life to come and visit us if the snobs keep making us do things their way?" Leticia asked. "I just—sometimes I could just strangle someone, I really could."

"I'm right there with you." Carter shrugged. "Sometimes you have to wonder why you took this sort of job."

"Maybe if I'd had any talent at it, I'd be one of those arrogant artists," Leticia said. "But I can't draw or sculpt or anything for shit. I just really, really love it."

"Same here. I mean, I never really tried that hard at actually making art. I just love talking about it and learning about it. It's like loving to watch movies but not actually wanting to help make one."

"Right! Exactly." Leticia grinned at him, glad that someone agreed with her and saw things the way that she did. "Oftentimes I feel like I'm dealing with people who have this job because they had no other choice, or they were artists who took it to have a steady paycheck and got stuck with it. But I chose this. I think art is worth protecting and sharing. If I can help do that, then I'm happy."

"I bet you were the sort of person who cried about the Nazi Devastation," Carter said.

"Oh God, yes. All the time. I saw that one film about it and they had this shot where they were burning a Picasso…"

"Yes!" Carter's eyes went wide. "I cried at that part, not gonna lie."

"It's just…" Leticia made a motion with her hands, unsure of how to say this. "I mean, everything is precious. But art—you can't replace art. It's unique. You can't—a car gets totaled, it's awful, but you can go and buy that same model. A house burns down, generally speaking it's not a very creative house, is it? You can rebuild it. But art, real art, you can't make it once it's gone. It's just… gone. We have to preserve it, whether it's a painting or an ancient city or whatever."

"You're straying dangerously close to the big 'what is art' question," Carter pointed out, the corners of his mouth twitching upward like he was trying not to smile. Carter struck her as the kind of guy who smiled easily. She liked that.

"Oh man." Leticia shook her head. "No, I am not getting into that argument again. Feels like that's half of what I'm doing, just arguing with people about what makes something art. I'll pass."

Mrs. Bunnag brought the check, which Carter insisted on paying and Leticia insisted on at least splitting. "Technically I'm your boss, you should be letting me pay for the entire thing."

"I'll let you split it," Carter replied. "But only because of that."

"Oh, please," Leticia snorted. "If I let you pay for all of it then it'll just convince Mrs. Bunnag this is a date."

"I have to admit, my heart pretty much stopped when I realized you were my coworker now. I felt so embarrassed."

"I know! My friends managed to get the story out of me last night and they teased me about it forever. As if either of us had any way of knowing who the other one was."

"Life likes to throw us these weird coincidences," Carter observed. "Sometimes it feels like the universe is laughing at me."

"Oh, definitely. Wait until you hear about what happened to my best friend, Sharon."

She told him all about how Sharon had met her husband Ross.

45

Sharon worked as the PR person for a local charity, one that Ross, a surgeon, donated to regularly. They met at a gala event and ended up having a one-night stand back at Ross's apartment. On her way home early in the morning, Sharon had gotten into a car accident.

"And the guy who operated on her…"

"Oh no way." Carter shook his head, laughing. "Seriously? Her one-night stand was her surgeon?"

"Now her husband," Leticia pointed out. "They're expecting their first kid."

"That is truly crazy." Carter indicated between them. "Ours really doesn't compare. They win."

"Thank you, that's what I said last night."

"You're being really great about this, though," Carter added. "Many people would have been cold or distant or maybe even nasty. You've been nothing but nice."

"Well it was hardly your fault," Leticia replied. "You didn't know any more than I did. And you've been pretty sweet about things yourself. And not just about this whole…" She waved between them. "Thing. Not every guy would be okay with having a woman as his boss."

"I assume you've earned it," Carter said. "And at the children's museum, most of my coworkers were women."

Leticia checked her watch. "Speaking of work, we should get back."

They finished paying and Leticia waved off Mrs. Bunnag with more insistence that Carter was *not* her boyfriend, just a coworker, of course she'd be back soon, maybe she'd bring Carter but maybe not because again, *not her boyfriend*, and then they were out the door.

"All of her kids are grown," Leticia observed. "And they don't live nearby. I think that her matchmaking me gives her something to do, you know? It's like having a child she can look after again."

"I get that," Carter said. "Parents just want the best for their kids, and she seems to think that being with someone is what would be best for you."

"I'm not disagreeing with her," Leticia replied. "I guess I've just never thought about it."

"About being with someone?"

"Well it's a perfectly nice idea," Leticia said, "But who's got the time? And where am I going to find someone who is willing to commit but also willing to go out and dance with me at a club when I want to work off some energy?" Not that she'd be going to clubs for too much longer. Already she was starting to feel a little old compared to most of the people who went there. She figured in another five years, she'd be done with them for good. Still, not like she was going to wait five years before finding a husband.

"Maybe the right person wouldn't ask you to make more time than you can give," Carter pointed out. "Or they'd find a way to spend time with you that didn't require you giving up any of yourself or what's important to you, like this job."

"You mean the job that's going to consume the rest of my life," Leticia joked. "Or at least that's how our old curator made it sound. I'm going to die an old maid at this rate."

"I'll be sure to give you a kitten to start your cat collection," Carter said solemnly.

Leticia laughed. "Don't you dare!"

"You don't like cats?" Carter put his hand over his heart. "I don't know if we can be friends."

"You look more like a dog person," Leticia commented.

"That's what everyone says." Carter heaved a sigh. "It's the great tragedy of my life."

"So are we friends?" Leticia asked, catching on to what he'd said a minute before.

"I'd like to be," Carter said carefully. "I mean, we have to spend a lot of time together. And we seem to get on well. I'd like us to keep being at least friendly with each other."

"No, I'd like that too, I just didn't know if… well, I mean—we slept together. I didn't know if that would color anything for you."

"Not in a negative way, at least," Carter replied, a hint of the flirtatious tones he'd used Friday night seeping in.

Leticia shivered just a little, thinking of all the things they'd done together on Friday. She definitely was thinking of him in a positive way—but also a not at all platonic way.

Still, he was her coworker. And she was his boss. If they were going to do anything more, he had to be the one to make the move, not her. If he didn't want to do that, if he just wanted to be friends, that was his choice. She would be fine with that.

And if she kept having vaguely inappropriate thoughts about taking him back to her office and ripping his shirt open and—

Well. She could handle those just fine.

CHAPTER 7

$\mathcal{M}$olly was exuberant after Carter picked her up from his parents' house. Working at the museum meant he couldn't pick her up directly after school, but it gave Molly a couple of hours with her grandparents every afternoon, so he was far from complaining.

"How did everything go today, Artemisia?" He asked, scooping her up in his arms and spinning her around.

Molly laughed. "Great! We got to learn about famous artists today! I get to do a paper on Picasso. Or, not a paper. We make this board with pictures and stuff on it."

"I'm sure you'll make a great one," Carter said, setting her down. "Do you have everything?"

"Yup!" Molly said, proud. She'd been scatterbrained when he'd first started her on this routine, always forgetting things at his parents' or at home or at school. Now she had it all handled.

Carter said a quick 'Hi' to Nan and Pops and then drove Molly home. A part of him wanted to just let him and Molly have dinner there, and sometimes they did, but he didn't want to become dependent on his parents. He'd been all right as a single parent, and as much as he appreciated Nan and Pops' help, he wanted to know that he was still Molly's primary caregiver.

"How is your new job?" Molly asked. "And your new boss? And the new museum? Can I visit it soon? What kind of art does it have?"

Molly had asked him similar questions before, and they'd visited the museum once or twice, but he had no problem explaining it again. "The new job is fine. It's very similar to my old one."

"Does this mean you have a cranky boss again?" Molly asked, wrinkling up her nose.

His last boss had been rather cranky. Oftentimes it had felt like no matter what he did, she would never be happy with it. When kids were involved, people tended to care more, but it also meant they were stricter about things. Everyone had their own opinions about what was good for the children, what the children deserved, and so on. Carter had a feeling that it was because when it came to children, everyone's instinct was to behave like a parent, and everyone parented differently.

"No, this boss is different." Carter tried to smother his grin, remembering Leticia. Leticia was as different from Diane as possible. Leticia was laid back and fun to spend time with, even if it wasn't strictly in a work capacity. Diane was straight laced to a fault and didn't seem to have a life outside of her job.

The fact that Leticia was gorgeous didn't help, either. Carter couldn't believe that she'd never been in a serious relationship. Sure, she was beautiful, all curves and light brown skin, but surely someone had to have seen the vivacious personality.

It made him a little angry, honestly, to think that all anyone had ever seen in her was a quick hookup.

Carter thought about that. If he was already getting protective of Leticia... Well, they were coworkers, yes, but surely they'd already proven how well they could get along. Maybe this was the perfect relationship to try for. He could go slow because of their work relationship, work himself up to a proper date instead of diving right in.

And he honestly liked Leticia. He wanted to spend more time with her. God knew he was still attracted to her. She'd been dressed professionally at work but he wasn't able to banish the image of her tight dress from the club or how she'd looked with nothing on at all.

He pulled into his driveway and helped Molly get out. "Can I do some drawing?" She asked.

"I don't know, have you finished your homework?" He replied.

Molly nodded solemnly. "Yes. I promise."

"Hey now, remember I told you, promises are for very big things only. You can't break a promise."

"Okay."

Carter had always tried to teach Molly the importance of that. Promises were giving your word, and that meant commitment. You didn't give that lightly.

"So, you did your homework. I suppose you can draw while I fix dinner. Spaghetti okay?"

"Okay!" Molly cried, dashing for the door and then racing upstairs. She didn't care what they ate for dinner when she got to do her drawing. Carter blamed it on having two parents that were invested in the arts, even if they couldn't do art themselves. Or maybe she'd gotten all the talent that he and Olivia hadn't had, like it had skipped a generation or something. Whatever the case, he tried to foster her desire to create art as much as he could.

On that note, maybe Leticia was also a good person to date because of her job. She loved art, he knew that. How could he be expected to date someone who didn't understand how much he loved art, who didn't appreciate it the way he did? How could he be with someone if they didn't agree with him on nurturing Molly's own artistic talent, making sure she got to explore it as much as she wanted?

And if he was being honest… he was kind of tired of mourning. Not that he didn't care about Olivia any more, but it was just—he was tired of missing her. It took so much time and energy, missing someone. It was a nice change to be excited for the day without feeling the weight of his loss hanging off of his shoulders.

He could still love Olivia, but he could remember the good things without focusing on the loss. He could move forward—and it was what she told him she wanted, time and again, when they knew it was the end. Not right away, of course, but she had wanted him to find happiness with someone again. Maybe now was the time, now that he could miss her without *missing* her, without actively mourning.

It felt like a weight that he hadn't even known he had was being taken off of his chest, piece by piece. Carter smiled privately down at the pasta bubbling on the stove.

Yes. Perhaps now was the time.

CHAPTER 8

*L*eticia entered the coffee shop, waving at Hal. "My usual!"

Hal shook her head. "You don't need it."

Leticia frowned. "Of course I need it." She narrowed her eyes. "Is this some misguided attempt to get me to cut down on my caffeine? Because I assure you—"

"No, she's referring to the fact that I already bought yours for you," Carter said from behind her.

Leticia jumped, turning around to see that Carter had, in fact, two coffees in his hand. "How do you know my coffee order?"

"Hal told me."

Leticia whipped back around, pointing accusingly at Hal. "Traitor!"

"He tips well," Hal replied, completely unabashed. "Maybe if you'd bribed me more often I wouldn't have sold you out."

"You're a horrible capitalist and your operas would have been shut down during the Stalin regime," Leticia declared.

But she turned and accepted the coffee from Carter, who was clearly trying not to laugh, while Hal spluttered about how that wasn't even really an insult, it was more like a compliment.

"What led to this?" She asked.

"I saw how much you need your coffee in the mornings, and I was stopping by here anyway, and I know that I tend to get here earlier than you do, so..." Carter trailed off. As he took a sip, Leticia noticed that the tips of his ears were pink.

She grinned to herself as she sipped her coffee.

Leticia had thought that it was a one-time thing, but then the next morning when she walked towards the coffee shop, Carter was emerging from it, two coffees in hand. She'd given him a suspicious glare but he'd just smiled at her and passed her the cup.

After a few days, she got used to it. She'd still say hello to Hal, maybe grab a pastry for dessert after lunch so she could ask the girl how'd she been doing and all, but in the morning she got used to Carter bringing her coffee.

He'd bring her some in the middle of the day sometimes too, when she'd been trapped in the office all day. Leticia wasn't sure what to think of it. Was this... was he courting her, for lack of a better word? Or was this just him being friendly? Maybe he'd done this for his previous coworkers as well.

What if this was his way of trying to win favor with her? She'd have thought that he didn't need to, with how friendly they'd gotten with one another and their relatively smooth start (even with the one-night stand). But maybe he saw it differently? Maybe he was still worried that she'd be angry somehow for how they'd met?

After about a week and a half of this, Leticia couldn't take it anymore. She had to ask and find out why Carter was going out of his way for her.

"All right," she said, taking the coffee. "What's going on here?"

Carter blinked at her. "You like coffee."

"Yes, we've established that I might be slightly addicted. Only slightly, whatever my friends may say. But why do you keep buying this for me?" Leticia realized that she probably sounded a little aggressive, and tried to soften it with a smile. "I appreciate it, I'm just curious."

She knew that Carter had to be going out of his way a little to give this to her. He hadn't frequented the coffee shop the first couple of days at work, and he had to bust his ass to get there before she did.

Carter shrugged. "It's not a problem, really. I need coffee, too. I know that you appreciate it and I like doing it for you."

Leticia stared at him for a moment. She knew that was a lie—or the part about it not being a problem, anyway. But he seemed really sincere about wanting to do it for her.

This was new. The idea that a guy would go out of his way to do something for her because he knew she liked it? And her liking it made it worth it for him? That had never happened to her before.

Leticia cleared her throat. "Look, if I'm wrong in what I'm about to say here, we can pretend I didn't say it. But... if this is what I think it is... don't you think that just asking me out on a date might have been easier?"

Carter ducked his head down, the tips of his ears turning pink again. Leticia smiled helplessly. He was adorable. "All right, so maybe I had a bit of an ulterior motive."

"You just couldn't get enough of all this, could you," Leticia said, teasing, gesturing at herself.

Carter arched an eyebrow and stepped a little closer, his gaze skimming over her body before dragging back up to look her in the eyes again. "Maybe," he admitted, his voice dropping down low and confident.

Leticia swallowed, her throat suddenly dry. The memory of their night together came rushing back. The way he'd ground into her on the dance floor. The way he'd gripped her and the confidence he'd had when he'd brought her to climax. She shivered and hastily took a sip of coffee to cover it up.

"And maybe I like the idea of you finally getting to go on a proper date," Carter added. His voice was still a little low, possessive. "Where you know you'll be more than just a hookup. Where I can treat you and help you feel taken seriously."

Oh, great, he had to be a gentleman about it, too. Leticia mentally decided that if he made good on that promise at their date, he'd be getting a blowjob at least.

"When are you taking me out, then?" She asked, taking a step forward of her own. The action nearly put them completely chest to chest, their coffee cups held awkwardly between them. She tipped her face up, close enough that he could kiss her if he wanted to.

She kind of wanted him to, even though they were near work and Hal was probably watching all of this through the window and grinning like a maniac. She knew the younger girl was rooting for them to get together. Not that Hal had been very subtle about it.

But there was no way that could actually happen. There were too many people who might see them that they worked with. The last thing she needed was for either her job or Carter's to be jeopardized because of an office romance.

Leticia stepped away reluctantly. She thought Carter understood why, because he gave a wry twist of his mouth before it slid into another grin.

"How about this Friday? That way if we end up hating each other we've got the weekend to get over it before we have to see each other again."

Leticia laughed. "That works for me. Although I doubt one date is going to make us hate each other if we've been doing this well so far."

"It has gone well, hasn't it?" Carter bumped his elbow against hers, conspiratorially. "So, since we work together and all, how about we just head out after work? Or do you want some time to get ready?"

Leticia thought about that. She generally stayed at work a little late on Fridays to wrap things up, so she had taken to bringing a clubbing outfit with her on those days so she could just change into it and head straight out from work. A date she could treat pretty much the same way.

"Sure, but I'm sure you've noticed I stay an hour late on Fridays. Is that okay?"

"That's totally fine. I could use the extra hour of work, too. I'm still getting into the swing of things."

"Perfect."

They started walking back towards the museum. "Any place in

particular that you have in mind?" Leticia asked, mentally going through her closet to figure out what to wear.

"Hey now, I can't tell you." Carter snorted. "That would be cheating."

"Oh c'mon." Leticia grabbed his arm, resting her head on his shoulder. "Please?" She pouted.

"Uh-huh. Your feminine wiles don't work on me. It's a surprise."

"You're awful," Leticia declared. "I don't know why I'm going out with you."

"Because I'm charming?" Carter suggested. "I played Prince Charming in my high school's production of *Cinderella*."

Leticia laughed. "Oh my God. I can totally picture that."

Carter seemed pleased that he'd made her laugh. "I'll have to see if my mom saved any photos. I'm sure she did. I thought I looked ridiculous in the outfit they put me in."

"You must have had all the girls," Leticia replied.

"Hardly, I was way too shy to ask anyone out," Carter admitted. "Oh, look, we're at work. I can dodge more questions about my awkward teenage years by doing my job."

"Just until Friday," Leticia promised him. "Then I can grill you all I want."

Carter laughed. "I'm looking forward to it."

She found that she was rather looking forward to it as well.

CHAPTER 9

Friday came and Carter found that he was more nervous than he'd been in a long time. Well, it stood to reason, didn't it? He hadn't been on a date since Olivia died.

But at the same time—well, he wasn't an idiot. He remembered well enough how dating went. Right? It was just like riding a bike. Or something. Right?

The point was, he should relatively know what he was doing on this. But it had been four years and—hell, actually, longer than that. He'd taken Olivia out on dates, of course. They'd made sure to take nights out for just the two of them. But this wasn't a sure-thing date. This wasn't a date with his wife or even a long-term girlfriend. This was a first date. And he hadn't been on one of those in... shit. He didn't even know how long. Not since he'd first asked Olivia out, anyway.

Even Molly could tell that something was up. When he'd said that her grandparents were going to come over and babysit her, she'd been pleased, especially when he'd suggested that if she kept behaving well for them he'd consider letting her go to sleepovers at her friends' houses. But her joy had been tampered by the serious way she'd watched him moving around, as if she were taking mental notes about him.

He'd thought he was home clear, but then that morning Molly had asked him what was wrong. "Is there something big at work?" She'd asked. "An exhibition coming in?"

She'd known that he always got a bit nervous before a new exhibition was set to come in and be unveiled. It was nerve wracking, making sure everything was set up properly and that nothing was broken, keeping the artist happy, making sure the public knew about it, that the donors and the board were all satisfied… Opening an exhibition always made his blood pressure spike.

"No, it's nothing like that," he'd told her. "I've just got an important meeting today."

"Okay." Molly nodded. Perhaps it was her mother's passing but, for all her childlike energy, she could also be rather serious and mature for her age. "I hope you do well, Daddy."

"Thanks, love."

Molly had been right though; he was terribly nervous. He felt like Leticia could pick up on it. He'd gotten her coffee as usual, Hal winking at him as she put in their order. He was pretty sure that Hal thought the two of them were already dating or something like that. When he'd handed the coffee over and they'd walked into work together, he'd felt normal. Like he could do this.

Then Leticia had spent all day being wrapped up in board meetings and he'd been running things on his end, mostly paperwork. It had meant that he hadn't really seen Leticia all day and that he'd been cooped up in his office without any other human interaction, all of which meant he had nobody to stop his mind from listing all of the ways that he could mess this up.

This shouldn't be such a hardship, right? He and Leticia had gotten along well so far. They'd been friendly and just barely flirting with one another, skirting the edge. He hadn't dared for much more, given that they were coworkers and had to be professional. But she'd figured out the coffee, in time, and he was sure she could still vividly remember their one night together the way that he could.

Still, he couldn't shake the fear that he was going to mess everything up, and that all that they'd been building towards would be ruined because he had forgotten how to properly date someone.

As it crept closer to the time they were supposed to head out, Carter forced himself to take a minute to make himself presentable. He'd brought an extra dress shirt and a tie and quickly freshened himself up in the restroom before changing. He was genuinely excited about where they were going. He hoped that Leticia felt the same.

Carter looked at himself in the mirror just before he emerged from the bathroom to go find Leticia. He looked good, he thought. More...formal than he liked to look. But this was a date, and Leticia was used to him looking formal. It was part of the job; you never knew when a board member or important donor was going to stop by the museum. Or when a tour guide would get sick and you'd have to give a tour at the last minute. All in all, he thought he looked nice.

Then he realized he had to get out of there before he started fiddling with his hair or something.

When he emerged from the bathroom, he saw that Leticia was just emerging from the women's restroom on the other side of the hallway. He instinctively gripped the handle of the door, staring.

Leticia wasn't wearing something as tight or revealing as the club, but it was still sexy. She was in a dress that had a flowing skirt, with a slit up the sides, revealing her stunning legs. The dress was a dark burgundy—it was the perfect fit for her personality and complemented her gorgeous skin color. The fabric draped over her top half, suggesting and following her curves without revealing too much, teasing him. Her hair was down in thick curls and her lipstick matched her dress.

She looked fabulous.

Carter felt like he'd been punched in the gut. He wanted to smear that lipstick. He wanted to see if she'd bruise the same color as her dress if he sucked hard enough at her pulse point. He wanted to slide his hands up her legs, part the fabric easily and make her wet, make her whimper.

He swallowed hard. Now was definitely not the time to be

thinking about things like that. First off, they were still at work. Technically, the museum was closed and he doubted they'd be needed for anything but, it was still work. He couldn't be doing anything inappropriate.

Second, he needed to focus if he was going to make it through the evening without tearing her clothes off. And he'd made a reservation and everything, so he wanted to get them to dinner on time.

Carter realized that Leticia hadn't noticed him yet, so he cleared his throat.

She jumped a little, then turned and smiled at him. He saw her gaze rake up and down his form appreciatively, and he was reminded of her saucy, aggressive grin in the nightclub. "Hey you," Leticia said, sauntering over—there was no word for it except 'saunter'—her hips swaying and that flirtatious smile still on her face.

"You ready to go?" he asked, smiling helplessly. He loved that she was this willing to be flirty, even when he didn't give her much back. His idea of flirting was just bringing her coffee and hoping for the best, for Christ's sake.

"Definitely. You?" Leticia seemed to approve of his outfit, if her giving him a once-over was any indication.

"Great. Let's lock up."

They locked up their offices, made sure that security knew that they were leaving, and then headed out to their cars. "I'll follow you there," Leticia said, getting into her car. She threw him a wink, though, and Carter wondered how she managed to make something so innocuous sound so flirtatious.

He tried to keep the pounding of his heart to a minimum as he drove to the restaurant. They parked in a parking garage nearby. This was partially because he had a second destination planned for after dinner and he didn't want Leticia to worry about having her car towed while he drove them to the next place, and partially because parking in a garage meant she still didn't know where they were going.

"All right," she said, emerging from her car next to him. "Time's up, cowboy. Where are we going?"

Carter offered his arm for her to take, feeling a rush of protective pleasure when Leticia took it, threading her arm through his. They started to walk out of the parking structure and down the street, the sky around them slowly falling into darkness.

"So, we met at a club," he said, "Which means I'm pretty sure you like dancing."

Leticia laughed. "Yeah, I think that's a pretty safe assumption."

"And I was thinking, of course we're hungry, so we want to eat," Carter went on, nerves hitting him and threatening to make him ramble. "But I didn't want to just do dinner. We've been getting lunch together when we can already. I want to shake things up. Make it special."

Leticia looked up at him, her cheeks going a little pink. "Thank you," she said, sounding surprised. Carter remembered what she had said about people just wanting to use her as a hookup. He felt a growl rise in his throat and had to swallow it down. Nobody deserved to be made to feel like they were only worth what their body could offer and nothing more. Especially not someone as vivacious and accomplished as Leticia.

Carter cleared his throat. "So I was thinking that we could get something to go along with our dinner. Like a show."

He pointed up at the building they'd just stopped at.

It had taken a fair bit of internet searching, but he'd found this great place that was a salsa club and restaurant. There was open dancing after a certain time of night and dance classes on some nights of the week. But there was also a specific time when a show was put on by the professional dancers. The food was said to be great, too.

"I didn't want to assume that you knew salsa or anything," Carter added. "I didn't think you'd know just because of your heritage or anything. I mean, I'm Irish and I can't do Irish dancing to save my life. But I thought it would be fun to watch either way."

"Oh my God," Leticia blurted out. She turned to him, eyes shining and a huge smile on her face. "I love this. I haven't done salsa dancing since I was—well, not for years. I'm awful. My cousins despair when I go home for Christmas."

"Home?"

"Mexico. Well, they're from Mexico. I was born here. But every year my parents would drag me and my siblings back—we'd bring Sharon with us, too. That was when we were in college, when she and her parents weren't in the best place in their relationship. But look at this!" Leticia laughed and threw her hand up at the building. "C'mon!"

She seized his hand and all but dragged him inside, grinning wildly like a kid who'd been taken to Disneyland.

Carter managed to pull her back a little so that he could speak to the hostess and ask for their reservation. They were led to a table just off to the side of the dance floor, where they could watch the dancing but still get a little bit of privacy. The dance floor was lit but the tables had dimmed lighting, created mostly by candles hanging from blown glass chandeliers in the ceiling.

He'd never claimed to be an expert on romance, but he liked to think that this might count as romantic. He definitely hoped that it counted as special.

Leticia sat down, still craning her head around to see everything. "They have a live band!" She grinned at him, a little giddy. "This is going to be great, thank you!"

She squeezed his hand before taking her menu to look at it, and Carter felt his chest fill with warmth. He was glad that Leticia was happy.

They ordered a couple of drinks but, almost immediately after, the music started up from the band. Several dancers swept onto the dance floor, which was a foot above the tables, allowing for a clear separation without it turning too much into a stage. Leticia clapped enthusiastically and cheered, which led to the people at the other tables laughing and cheering.

The music paused momentarily, a tension-filled pause indicating the start of the show. Everyone held their breath—and then the music started up again and the dancers began to move.

Carter knew he should have been watching the dancers. And he was, glancing their way as they swirled around each other, hips rotating and feet tapping, but his eyes were drawn to Leticia. She was watching the dancers with rapt attention, her eyes a little wide in a happy way, like when Molly watched fireworks.

He liked the idea of doing this for Leticia again and again—well not this, specifically, but different things, anything that would make her happy and enraptured like this. She deserved it.

He'd seen how she stayed an hour late every night, even now that he was getting into the swing of things with his new job. She was the one who dealt with the board and donors, more than he did, and she was the one who took responsibility for everything. She had to make sure she coordinated with security, that the art was being properly taken care of, and that all the programs the museum ran were going smoothly. No wonder she'd convinced herself that she hadn't found time for a proper relationship.

Carter disagreed. He thought that Leticia could still have a proper relationship with someone. That someone just needed to show her that she was worth a little extra effort. Someone who understood how hard she worked and didn't pitch a fit at her schedule.

And, well… Why shouldn't that person be him?

He wanted to be the one to show her that her life wasn't too much for someone to handle. She didn't have to wait until things died down or until she was working a less demanding job. He had plenty of demands on his time as well. He could certainly understand.

The waiter came up as they were watching the dancing, and they quickly ordered. The food was delicious, but the dancing was still going, so they didn't talk about it much. The dance show ended about halfway through their meal and they finally got a chance to talk.

The music continued, lower this time, and a few couples got onto the dance floor. Now that the show was over, the restaurant was adjusting so that you weren't being as forcefully directed to watch the dance floor. Carter turned to Leticia, waiting patiently as she slowly came back to herself.

She blinked at him, and then down at her food, which she'd sort of just been picking at. "Oh man. That was so much fun to watch. I almost wanted to join them." She quickly wolfed down some of her food to make up for ignoring it before.

"I wish I could dance like that," Carter said.

"You were pretty good at the club," Leticia pointed out. "I'm sure I could teach you how to salsa, if you wanted."

"You've got to be as good as those dancers, right?"

Leticia shook her head. "Not necessarily. My cousins are all really good at it, but they go out to that sort of dancing all the time. I'm much better at club dancing. They always tease me about it, because salsa actually originated in New York City. It was picked up by Mexico and other Latin countries after the fact. They say that, since I'm the American, I should know it better than they do."

"I didn't know that," Carter said honestly. He'd had no idea.

"Yeah, most people think it originated somewhere in South or Central America, and I mean, the people who came up with it were Puerto Ricans so it's an understandable assumption."

"How many cousins do you have?" Carter asked.

"Oh man." Leticia thought for a moment. Finally she rolled her eyes good-naturedly. "I don't even remember. My mom has four brothers, and my dad has two sisters and a brother, and each of them has at least three kids. And a couple of them have kids, since they're all around my age. So, there's a lot of us." She shrugged. "Hispanic Catholics, what are you gonna do?"

"Irish Catholics," Carter said, "Although my parents are really lazy about it. My mom's side of the family is pretty much nonexistent at this point, but my dad has three brothers so I've got nine cousins on that side of the family."

"Any siblings?" Leticia asked.

Carter shook his head. "Only child. Sometimes I was a little envious of the other kids. They always had someone on their side, y'know? I mean, half the time they seemed to hate their siblings but, if they were in a pinch, they had someone to spend time with or someone who'd have their back. But I also liked it. I got my parents' full attention. And I was never lonely, exactly. I think it helped that I was a real bookworm."

"I've got two younger brothers," Leticia said. "Twins. One's in law school and the other's getting his medical degree. They've always been such overachievers."

"Says the head curator for our museum."

Leticia blushed a little. "Fair, I suppose, but they were always the ones who had these big dreams. I remember Julio wanted to be the president at one point. I just wanted to take care of art. My cousins aren't lazy or uneducated, not at all, but we all like to tease the twins. They can get a bit too ambitious for their own good."

"Sounds like you guys all get along pretty well."

"Yeah, I was lucky. My parents and I have had our rough patches but it's never been too bad."

"My parents and I were always close. They've really been great and let me depend on them when I needed it, including emotionally."

"Yeah, they're great to turn to during those rough patches."

Carter wanted to tell her—it was on the tip of his tongue—but habit made him hold back. This was only their first date. They'd gotten to know each other at work, sure, but it wasn't the same thing as openly stating romantic interest.

And besides, how did one even say, "Oh yeah, one real rough patch was when my wife died"?

Instead, he swallowed his words and nodded along. There was plenty of time to tell her later, if this date went well and they became more serious. There was no need to rush things.

From there, the talk turned to art, and how they had each gotten into it.

"My mom was a volunteer tour guide," Carter explained. "She would help with taking people around museums, usually groups of school kids. She didn't have a formal education in the subject or anything, she just wanted to give back to the community and that seemed like a fun way to do it. Through that, she started watching documentaries on famous artists and buying books about them and stuff and, like I said, I was a bookworm. Those were the books around the house, so I read them, and I ended up falling in love with art."

"I remember the moment it happened for me," Leticia said. "We were going to the local museum for a school field trip and we attended this exhibit about how different religions, like say the Crusades, would obliterate each other's art. And I remember standing there, hearing about how these precious works were destroyed and could never be replaced or recovered—and it just filled me with such anger. I think it amused my teacher. But from that moment, I knew I wanted to have a job to protect art so that would never happen again."

Leticia gave a small laugh. "When I was a kid, of course, this meant I was going to become a high-end art thief. Obviously. Like some kind of art world version of Robin Hood. I was determined to find art that was lost or stolen or in the wrong hands and return it."

"Oh man, where were you for the Steward Gardner Museum robbery?"

"It drives me nuts that those thieves are still at large!" Leticia exclaimed, leaning in. "They cut the pictures out of the frames. They irreparably damaged those priceless works of art! And for what? Those paintings aren't worth as much if they're damaged, they had to know that!"

Carter started laughing. He couldn't help it—he was pissed about the theft too, and the fact that the thieves had never been caught and the paintings had been damaged was awful. But Leticia spoke with such righteous anger and conviction that he was charmed. He would love to sic her on some of the PTA moms at Molly's school.

"Sorry," he said, "I'm not laughing at you. I just—you're so passionate. I love it."

"I know, I'm a walking cliché," Leticia replied. "The passionate Latina."

"Hey, I'm not complaining." Carter grinned. "I love it. I feel like so many of us have this pressure to be academic and all formal and stuff, when it's okay to get passionate."

"Get passionate, huh?" Leticia winked at him, slow and sly, and Carter could feel his skin heating up.

The waiter came by, checking on the food and asking if they wanted dessert, but Carter's mind was already going to dirtier places. Like eating Leticia for dessert.

Some of what he was thinking must have shown on his face,

because Leticia asked for dessert but gave him a smoldering look the moment the waiter disappeared. "I hope you don't have any plans to go home early tonight."

"Actually," Carter said, "There's something after dinner."

"You've got to be kidding me." Leticia laughed. "I'm surprised, in a good way, but also I really want to yank that tie off of you."

"Patience is a virtue," Carter told her, even though he really liked the idea of taking her back to the parking garage and seeing how far back the seats on his car could go. But he wanted to show her the next bit of the evening—if it hadn't gotten too late.

Fortunately, by the time they finished dessert, they still had time for his second activity. When he'd been looking up the restaurant-slash-dance club, and called them up to make a reservation, the hostess had informed him that it would be wise to arrive a little early if he wanted good parking.

"There's an art fair opening that evening that goes through the weekend," she'd explained. "It's the anniversary of something or other in World War II and all of the work is by Jewish artists. It's a big deal, so there might not be a lot of parking spaces left if you come later in the evening."

Carter had thanked her for the tip, and that was how he'd figured out the second part of the evening.

Besides, maybe walking off some of that wine and massive enchilada was a good idea.

"I get the check this time," he said, teasing about their usual argument over lunch about who was paying for whom this time.

Leticia sighed dramatically. "I suppose that's acceptable, just this once."

Afterwards, Carter offered her his arm again.

"I feel a little like I'm in a regency drama," Leticia commented. "Not that I'm complaining or anything. But holding open doors, offering me your arm..."

"I know. I'm the last of a dying breed." Carter grinned at her, then indicated the path ahead of them. "Would you like to take a short walk?"

"Sure…" Leticia said, suspicion in her voice. "Does this have anything to do with the second activity that's keeping me from mind-blowing sex?"

Carter could feel himself getting flushed with embarrassment. He liked that Leticia was so forthright and honest about sex, that she was open about her desires and where she wanted the evening to go, but he was also unused to it. It had been a long time since anyone had openly stated how much they wanted him. It caught him off guard to remember that he could be seen as attractive, as someone sexual.

He'd gotten a taste of that in the club, of course, on their first night. But wasn't nearly anyone attractive in the club? Even people who weren't there for sex caught onto the vibe of it. Clubs were as much about sex as they were about alcohol and dancing. But Leticia was still flirting with him and still clearly wanted him, even in the light of day and not in some dark club with the bass thumping.

It made him respond in kind, made him want to slide his hands all over her and make her beg for him.

But first, the art fair.

He knew that Leticia would appreciate any art fair, of course, but after she'd admitted that she'd cried over the Nazi theft of all the art, he thought that she would especially appreciate a fair focusing on celebrating local Jewish artists.

Judging by the look on her face when she saw the sign at the entrance to the art fair, he'd guessed rightly.

Leticia let out a small "oh," and turned to smile at him, eyes shining all over again. "Carter, seriously, this is super sweet."

Carter shrugged, feeling self-conscious. He wanted her to feel special, he didn't think that he should be the one getting attention. This was about giving Leticia a night that would make her happy.

"It's really nothing," he said, deflecting.

Leticia got up onto her tiptoes and gave him a quick kiss on the cheek. "It's definitely not just nothing," she said, smiling. "But thank you. Nobody's ever made an effort like this for me."

"Well it's about time somebody did," he told her, meaning it.

"And you're getting properly rewarded for it later, no worries," Leticia replied.

Carter had to swallow hard against the desire to slide his hand into her hair and kiss her obscenely, messily, right there in front of everybody. "You really shouldn't say things like that," he warned her.

"But why?" Leticia replied, her face and voice giving him the picture of innocence. "It makes you look so damn hot and your ears turn a lovely shade of pink."

He growled low in his throat and used her arm, looped through his, to pull her flush against him. "Careful, missy, you're playing with fire here."

"Perfect." Leticia leaned in, her gaze searching his. "I want to get burned."

Then she yanked herself free and darted away from him, laughing, hurrying to wander through the art fair.

Carter had to jog a little to catch up with her, looping an arm around her shoulders like it was the most natural thing in the world. He didn't even think about it until he'd already done it and he almost froze up. He'd often done the same thing with Olivia, dropping an arm around her shoulders and tucking her into his side. He had just dropped back into that habit with Leticia, when she might not welcome constant physical contact. She might not want such an overly romantic gesture.

But Leticia just snuggled up into his side and guided him through the fair. Mostly she did this by pointing at whatever booth she wanted to investigate next. She would talk with all of the stall owners animatedly and tuck their business cards and flyers into her purse. And she was constantly sighing over this or that art piece that she wanted to buy but couldn't.

"If I bought every piece of art that I wanted to, I'd be broke within a week," she announced. "And I can't buy anything right now. I'm not making you lug it around for the night and I've got a different goal in mind for this evening."

"I wonder what that goal could possibly be," Carter replied,

"Seeing as you've been so coy with me all evening about what you want."

Leticia giggled. "Hey, I wouldn't have gotten far in life if I hadn't learned how to state my intentions and ask for what I want."

"Fair enough. And for the record, I like it."

Leticia bit her lip. "Really?" She asked. "It's not—I'm not too... aggressive?"

"I think I can handle whatever you throw at me," Carter replied.

"You can handle me anytime," Leticia promised.

"And besides, it's flattering," he admitted. "I haven't dated in a while. It's nice to be reminded that people find me attractive."

"Trust me, I'm not the only one who finds you attractive, I'm sure," Leticia assured him. She paused, looking around them at the booths. "I love this, but this fair is supposed to be here all weekend and I'm very impatient."

"Whatever for?" Carter asked. "It's not like we've been hinting at sex all night or anything."

Leticia playfully glared at him. "Just for that, I'm going to make you race me to my apartment."

Carter nodded. "Challenge accepted."

They walked back to their cars, where Leticia gave him the address and they got into their cars at the same time. Then, they raced.

Or as much as anyone can race in two cars while also obeying all traffic laws and not speeding.

Leticia got there first, undoubtedly because she knew shortcuts to her apartment and didn't have to rely on a map app on her phone like Carter did. But he was certain that she'd only beaten him by a minute at the most.

He pressed the button to ring for her apartment. "Who is it?" Leticia asked, her voice floating teasingly over the line.

Carter leaned in and lowered his voice. If she could be a little aggressive, then so could he. "Unlock this door so I can come upstairs and make you scream," he told her, all but growling the words.

He could have been mistaken, given the crappy quality of the intercom, but he thought he heard an aroused gasp from the other end of the line. A second later, the door buzzed to indicate that it was unlocked, and he flung it open. He took the steps two at a time, not even bothering with the elevator, too busy thrumming with energy.

When he reached Leticia's floor, he took a moment to catch his breath, think of what he was going to do, what the plan was. Then he straightened himself up, crossed the last few feet to her door, and knocked.

Leticia—who had taken advantage of her head start to change, apparently—opened the door almost immediately. She was now wearing a thin periwinkle nightgown that barely covered her ass and thighs, clinging to her curves. He could see her nipples pushing out against the thin fabric and the tops of her breasts moving with her harsh, anticipatory breaths.

He'd liked the dress she was wearing but this—this was unbearable. A man only had so much patience when there was a barely-wrapped present like this waiting for him, within arm's reach.

Leticia raked her gaze over him. "Well?" She asked, her voice soft but challenging. "I thought you were going to make me scream."

He gave a sound that he couldn't even name, half growl and half something else, maybe even a snarl, and then he was striding into the apartment and closing the door behind him.

Leticia stood firm, her lips parting on a sharp intake of breath as he grabbed her and hauled her against him. He slid a thigh between her legs and palmed her ass, remembering how it had felt to dance with her like this at the club.

"Oh God," Leticia gave a little gasp, her hands coming up to clutch at his chest. "Carter, please—"

"Are you wet already?" He asked, jolting his thigh and making Leticia moan a little. "You are, aren't you?"

She nodded, biting her lip as he jolted his thigh again. He moved one of his hands up to her waist to haul her closer to him and kiss the life out of her.

Leticia melted against him, her hands tightening in the fabric of his shirt and opening up for him easily. He slid his tongue into her mouth over and over again, deep and filthy, while he guided her into grinding down onto his leg with his hand on her ass.

"That's it," he commanded, kissing along her throat. "Get yourself good and wet for me."

Leticia all but writhed on his leg at that, making a desperate noise. Carter grinned. "Does that mean you like dirty talk? Would you like it if I told you to work yourself faster?"

"Y-yes," Leticia stuttered.

"What else do you like?" He asked, lightly pinching her nipple through the fabric of her negligee.

"I—keep talking dirty to me, tell me what you want to do to me."

He kissed her again, quick and dirty, then yanked her negligee up over her head and tossed it aside. He liked that she was naked now and he was still clothed, at least for now. "You want me to tell you about how I'm going to pin you down to this bed and finger you until you're begging for me?" He asked.

Leticia looked like her knees almost buckled at that. She lunged for him, kissing him frantically and yanking at his tie and shirt until she was nearly popping buttons off. Carter pulled away a little to help her, chuckling at how quickly he could get her frantic. He was feeling a little frantic himself, desperate to get inside of her, but he wanted to drive her insane first. He wanted her to beg him to slide inside of her and fuck her senseless.

Maybe it just the fact that it had been a while since he'd slept with anyone, but he couldn't recall ever being so desperate for another person. He wanted to watch as Leticia screamed her climax, he wanted his hands and mouth on every inch of her, and he wanted her hands and mouth all over him in turn.

Leticia kissed her way down his chest, sinking to her knees, derailing any other thought. "Been wanting to taste you for so long," she whispered, her voice husky, as she undid his belt.

Carter shivered as she yanked down his pants and took him into her hand, sighing as she felt him go from half hard to fully hard. Carter tried to keep his hips from thrusting into her touch. It never felt as good when he did this himself—he loved the feel of a smaller, softer hand on him, and Leticia was very, very good at this.

Then she started licking at the head, and Carter swore loudly. Leticia laughed low in her throat, and then she was licking a long wet stripe up the underside of him.

Carter slid his hands into her hair, shaking a little with the effort of keeping himself still as Leticia took him fully into her mouth. She worked her way further and further down onto him, until he could feel himself almost hitting the back of her throat. He groaned, shuddering as Leticia fluttered her tongue around the head and added just the fainted scrape of teeth.

"Good girl," he mumbled, almost subconsciously. "You'll take it all eventually, won't you?"

Leticia shuddered at that, and Carter saw her knead one of her own breasts, lightly flicking the nipple. He grinned. "Oh, you like praise, do you? Want me to tell you how good you are sucking my cock? How it feels like you were made for it?"

She groaned around him, the vibrations making him swear and tighten his fingers in her hair.

Leticia whined and abruptly slid a hand between her legs, pressing hard at her clit. Carter tugged hard on her hair. "Nuh-uh. You don't get to touch yourself. I do. You're a good girl and you'll do whatever I want you to do, isn't that right?"

Leticia moaned around him but pulled her hand away, obeying him. "Good girl."

He tightened his grip on her hair and pulled her off of him, ignoring the annoyed look that she sent him.

"Now, now, I still have to make good on my promise, don't I?" He smiled down at her, half wondering where this confidence had come from and half turned on out of his mind with the image before him: Leticia on her knees, precum slicking up her lips, her hair messy, panting desperately for him.

He helped her to her feet and kissed her, licking the taste of himself from her mouth. He flexed his fingers into her hips and Leticia ground up against him, arching her back like a cat in heat.

Abruptly he turned her around, placing a palm between her shoulder blades to gently push her down onto the bed. "Spread your legs."

Leticia did as he asked, visibly shivering.

"Good," he crooned, bracing himself over her. "Such a good girl for me

"Please," Leticia said, arching up towards him. "Touch me, please, please—"

Well, who was he to argue when she begged so prettily?

Carter stepped out of his pants and then slid an arm around her middle, pulling her back flush to his chest. Then he slid a hand between her legs and slowly began to bear his weight down on her, until she was almost completely pressed down into the mattress.

His first touch to her clit had Leticia moaning again, her nails digging into the sheets. He didn't waste a moment, working her hard and fast—quick, dirty circles until she was making little gasping noises and grinding down into his hand.

"That's it, work yourself on it, so desperate for it like this," he gasped, so incredibly turned on. He slid a finger inside of her and Leticia sobbed, her hips thrusting desperately. "You want it so badly, don't you? Such a good girl, fucking yourself on my fingers."

"More," Leticia begged. "More, I want more, please—"

"More?" Carter slowed down a little and Leticia let out a cry of frustration. "Greedy little thing, aren't you? You want me to let you fuck my fingers until you come?"

"Yes," Leticia gasped.

"And why is that? Why do you want me to let you do that?"

"Because—because I'm a good girl," Leticia admitted, sounding incredibly turned on to say such a thing out loud. "Because I want it."

Carter groaned, painfully hard. "That's right," he told her, sliding in another finger as a reward. "Good girl."

He started fingering her harder, no longer teasing, just doing his best to drive her crazy. Leticia was leaning her full weight against his arm now, her hips thrusting impatiently as she chased her orgasm.

Carter let her, slipping in another finger, working her until she was good and wet and almost out of control.

Then he slid his fingers out of her and, with no warning, began rubbing furiously at her clit with two of his fingers. Leticia screamed, her body jerking frantically, Carter's hand and wrist becoming slick with her juices as she came, thrashing in his arms.

"Good girl," he murmured, kissing her just behind her ear. God, he couldn't wait to get inside of her.

"Get inside me," Leticia begged. She twisted around, her hands grabbing for him wildly, trying to pull him to her. "Oh my God, fuck, please, get inside me and fuck me, Carter!"

Well, he wasn't about to say no to that.

He crawled on top of her and pressed her down into the mattress, using his knee to kick her leg wide. Leticia pushed herself up onto her elbows and grabbed him by the shoulders, drawing him down to her. She kissed all over his chest and shoulders, frantic, mumbling out little begging phrases in between like, "please," and "you'll feel so good, I'll make it so good," and "I need it so bad."

Carter grabbed a condom out of his wallet where he'd stashed it this morning and slicked himself up, squeezing himself hard at the base of his cock so that he wouldn't come too soon. Leticia was still grabbing at him impatiently, so he started to enter her—slowly, just in case. He didn't want to hurt her and it was better safe than sorry until he got used to all the particular quirks of Leticia's body.

Leticia didn't appreciate this too much, and she quickly made that fact known by hooking one leg over his shoulder and then grabbing the other and pulling it up until her leg was folded flat against her chest.

Carter nearly choked on his own spit and his hips stuttered, sliding him the rest of the way in. Leticia moaned in appreciation, thrusting up a little to meet him.

Holy shit. Carter hadn't been with anyone this flexible since his high school girlfriend, who'd also been on the gymnastics team. "Jesus Christ," he blurted out, tucking his face into the crook of Leticia's neck and trying desperately to remember how to breathe. She was so hot and tight around him and he was shaking with the effort of holding back and letting her adjust to him.

After a moment or two, Leticia started to grind against him, trying to thrust properly but unable to because of her current position. Carter kissed her quickly on the neck to show that he understood and began to drive into her, hard and desperate, unable to be slow or careful any longer. Leticia, thank God, seemed to like it, gasping and doing her best to meet him thrust for thrust even when she could do little more than writhe.

"That's it," he gasped, as Leticia wrapped a hand around the back of his neck and started whimpering. He was so close, but he didn't want to finish without Leticia coming a second time. He took her hand, which was digging into his arm, and guided it down between her legs.

"Make yourself come for me," he ordered, his voice hoarse. "C'mon, I want to see you one more time, I want to see your face."

Leticia started fingering herself desperately. She pried her eyes open and looked down between them and let out a little moan. Carter looked down as well and saw what she was looking at: the sight of his cock sliding in and out of her.

He had to slam his eyes closed and bite his tongue hard not to come right away at the sight of that. He increased his pace even more and leaned down to kiss Leticia, stealing the breath right from her mouth.

She cried out into the kiss and he felt her fingers pause as she clenched madly around him and came. That was more than he could handle and he stiffened, shuddering as he came so hard he almost collapsed on top of her.

Carter slid out of her and fell onto his side, narrowly avoiding falling on her. He had felt that orgasm all the way down to his fingertips. Next to him, Leticia seemed to be gasping to get her breath back, her body shaking slightly.

He reached over, pushing her hair out of her face and gently stroking her cheek. "You were beautiful," he told her, and he meant it. He leaned in and kissed her quickly on the lips before settling back.

Leticia smiled at him, looking a little dazed but also a little surprised.

"What is it?" He asked. He propped himself up on his elbow to look down at her.

Leticia shrugged, letting him continue to stroke her skin but looking down and away from him. "It's just—I'm a little kinky in bed, in case you can't tell. For most guys, that translates to—I don't know. Like, they think that just because I like things a certain way during sex, I'm going to want to be treated like nothing once we're done, when that's not it at all. And they just, y'know, thank me and leave."

Carter felt a quick punch of guilt—because he did have to leave soon. He couldn't spend the night, not when his parents were expecting him. If he stayed away all night, Molly would be sure to notice, and he didn't know how to explain to her yet. How could he explain to a seven-year-old what 'casual dating' was? No, he'd have to wait until he was more serious with Leticia, if he ever got serious with Leticia, to talk to Molly about it.

But he didn't want Leticia to think that he was abandoning her.

"Well, sounds like you had some crappy guys," he said. "No offense meant towards your taste or anything."

Leticia shrugged. "I know. Anyway. You're very sweet. I appreciate that." She laughed ruefully. "And you're also kinky, who knew?"

"I hardly call a little dirty talk all that kinky," Carter pointed out.

"True, you should hear some of the stuff my friend Sharon and her husband get up to."

"I'm not sure I want to hear. Unless you're offering suggestions for next time."

Leticia looked up at him and for the first time, she actually looked shy. She was blushing slightly as she looked up at him through her lashes. "You'd like for there to be a next time?"

"Sure." Carter frowned. "Unless you don't want there to be."

"No, I do want." Leticia rolled onto her side and smiled brightly at him. "In that case, there are a few suggestions that I have."

Carter laughed tiredly. Smiling, he said, "Of course, this woman has stipulations… I can't wait to hear them." Just so long as she didn't send them to him in a work email or something like that. He didn't know if he'd be able to stand that, thinking about fucking Leticia while she was only one room away and completely untouchable because, you know, professionalism.

And now... came the awkward part.

He stroked down Leticia's back until she was relaxed and her eyes were obviously heavy, her blinks getting slower and lazier as time went on. Then he carefully got out of bed and padded over to the bathroom. There was a washcloth on the side of the sink. He grabbed it, got it under warm water, and then returned, carefully wiping Leticia down and disposing of the condom in the trash.

As he started to get his clothes back on, Leticia stirred from her post-orgasm dozing.

"You're leaving?" Leticia asked. She sounded confused. Carter couldn't really blame her for it.

"Unfortunately." He gave her what he hoped was a reassuring smile. "I've got an early morning tomorrow, sorry."

It was the same excuse he'd given her last week, if he remembered correctly. He wondered how long he could use that until she started to get suspicious.

"Okay," Leticia said. She still sounded confused and not completely satisfied with his answer, but she didn't push him on it.

"Sleep well, okay?" He finished pulling his shirt on and leaned over to kiss her one last time. This time the kiss was soft, one of those slow pulling kisses—the kind that he'd only had with long-term girlfriends.

He tried not to think about that too much. Instead he just pushed her hair back out of her face and dropped a last kiss to her cheek before slipping out the door.

It didn't help that a part of him really did want to stay. Post-sex Leticia was all pliant, heavy limbs and sweet laziness, a huge differ-ence from her usual self. Not that he didn't like her normal bluntness and exuberance, but he liked this other side of her, too. He wanted to get to know it better. And what better way than to stay, wrap her up in his arms, see what she was like in the morning? He knew that he'd enjoy waking up with her, making her pancakes and orange juice and maybe getting in some relaxing, fun shower sex or something before he headed out.

But that wasn't possible. His parents were waiting for him and he couldn't expect them to stay up too late, not at their age, and Molly—he couldn't change things up on Molly too suddenly.

He only hoped that Leticia's confusion wouldn't morph into unhappiness. He didn't know how he could begin to explain his life to her. Not when things were so new. And he couldn't risk Molly getting hurt.

Carter decided that he would deal with all of this if Leticia brought it up. In the meantime, he was going to go home, thank his parents, and hug his little girl and put her to bed.

This thing with Leticia though... Carter grinned as he got into his car.

Damn. Sexy as hell, a little bit kinky, honest and intelligent, and for some reason totally into him.

He wasn't sure what he'd done to land such a catch but he was damn sure going to do what he could to see where this was going.

CHAPTER 10

*L*eticia tapped her foot, an old nervous habit she hadn't had since her senior year finals. She'd been panicking, worried that she'd flunked her math elective and was going to have to stay an extra semester just to make that one damn class up.

She understood that it wasn't a big deal that Sharon was five minutes late. God knew that she had plenty on her plate already. But on today of all days, Leticia did not need one more thing to stress her out. Not when she was already working herself up into a tangle.

Sharon finally ran up, or ran as much as a pregnant woman could, plopping herself down in the seat across from Leticia. "Jesus Christ, driving while pregnant is the most annoying thing ever. Remind me that if we want a second kid after this that I'm adopting, okay? I don't care what I say, remind me how my feet swelled up and I couldn't sleep on my stomach and how awful driving was, and that I made you promise me you'd make me adopt."

"Okay," Leticia said slowly. "Do you need a couple of minutes?"

"Nah, just some water."

Leticia signaled the waiter. She was meeting Sharon at a small diner halfway between their respective offices. It meant she was taking a slightly longer lunch but, screw it. She was the head curator

—she could pull some privilege every once in a while. She was the boss and she'd earned it, damn it.

After water was delivered, Sharon took a big gulp and then fixed her eyes on Leticia. Her stare said that she knew that something was up. "I'm assuming there's a reason you took some precious time out of your workday, now that you're all high and mighty, to talk to me. While I'm about to go on maternity leave and have to make sure everything's set for while I'm gone, by the way."

"I know, I know, and I'm sorry."

"Letty, I'm not upset. If I was, I would tell you. I'm just pointing out that you know how much time this takes out of both of our days, and I know that you know, which means that I know something's up." Sharon leaned in, taking Leticia's hand. "Are you okay? What's wrong?"

Leticia shook her head. "Nothing's wrong, I promise. I just wanted to talk through some things with you."

"Okay." Sharon still looked suspicious but she sat back. "And I presume you want me nice and buttered up for this, which is why you chose a diner with delicious, greasy food that I currently can't resist."

"You would presume correctly," Leticia replied. She sighed. "Look, I might be acting like a complete idiot here."

"You're talking to the woman who got engaged after only a couple of months of dating," Sharon pointed out. "And I was banging my doctor. I'm not exactly in a position to judge."

"Actually, according to the ruling of the medical board…"

"Oh Lord." Sharon rolled her eyes, but she had a fond smile on her face. "If you'd told me at the time that there would come a day when I'd be joking about that entire mess, I'd have told you to stick it where the sun didn't shine."

"Time softens a lot of things," Leticia commented. Then she sighed and got down to business. "Okay. So. The guy that I slept with a month ago."

"Which guy, you always—" Sharon paused. "Wait."

Leticia watched as her friend sat back, folding her arms over her large stomach. "You haven't mentioned any guys," she said, her tone wondering. "Normally you've got one every weekend, but you haven't mentioned anyone since..."

The realization dawned on Sharon's face. Her jaw went slack and her eyes widened, shining with understanding. "Not since the guy who turned out to be your new coworker!"

Leticia nodded. "Yup."

Sharon sat up straight. "Wait. Wait, the guy—you didn't—you two aren't..." She looked Leticia directly in the eye. "Letty."

Leticia cleared her throat. "Yes. Well. Um. We try not to do anything at the museum? If that helps?"

"You're fucking your coworker!" Sharon whispered fiercely. "Oh my God, Letty! You're—he's not even your coworker. Technically, you're his boss—Jesus fucking Christ!"

"Say it a little louder, why don't you?" Leticia hissed. "I don't think those octogenarians in the back of the diner heard you, what with their needing hearing aids and all!"

"Sorry, sorry," Sharon said, lowering her voice. "I cannot believe this, Leticia. You're actually sleeping with a coworker? Do you have any idea how messy that can be?"

"It's been working out so far and it's been almost a month," Leticia pointed out.

"Are you two..." Sharon waved her hand vaguely in the air. "Y'know."

"Having sex?" Leticia asked, deadpan. "Yes, fairly regularly, sometimes with handcuffs."

Sharon huffed. "That's not what I'm asking." She paused. "Wait. Is this what you set this up to talk about? You're boning your coworker?"

"First of all, who uses the term 'boning' anymore?" Leticia asked. "And... yes. Okay. I'm having a bit of a crisis."

"I should imagine so," Sharon snorted. "If your boss finds out, you're going to get your ass whipped and not in the fun way."

"Hardy har har. You think I don't know that? I looked it up, there's no policy against coworkers dating or anything like that."

"You'd think there would be."

"This is an art museum, it's not like inter-office romances are a big thing to worry about when you've got, say, an entire country in Europe breathing down your neck because you're holding an exhibition starring some of their prized artwork by their prized artists."

"Fair point."

"So." Leticia took a deep breath. She had to get this over with quickly or she'd never be able to get it all out.

She started by explaining the awkward meeting, and then how she and Carter had worked to be friendly. She talked about their workplace lunches. How easily they got along. She even talked about how Mrs. Bunnag was convinced that they were dating (even before they'd slept together the second time).

Then the coffee had started, and after about a week and a half of it, she'd realized that this was his way of flirting and doing something nice for her. She'd told him to ask her on a date, and he had, and they'd gone out for a dinner at a salsa dancing club and then a walk through an art festival for Jewish artists.

"Sounds like he knows you really well," Sharon interrupted gently. Or perhaps shrewdly, going by the light in her eyes. "I mean, that sounds like the perfect night for you. Dancing, dinner, and a walk through an art festival? And one that counteracts the one event in history that makes you cry?"

"Oh, shut up, I wasn't the only one crying in that one history class."

"We were crying at the mustard gas images, Letty. You were crying because a statue got smashed."

Leticia waved it off. "Anyway."

She explained how they'd gone back to her place and had amazing sex—and how he was still sweet afterwards, not treating her like trash just because he'd discovered she liked to be called names a bit during sex.

"But he didn't stay?" Sharon asked, confirming.

Leticia nodded. "He didn't stay the first time, either."

"I can understand that, though. You never stayed over the few times you went over to some other guy's place, y'know?"

"Right, we didn't know each other then, so it was... I mean it was disappointing but not out of the ordinary. But the second time..."

"And did he stay over any other times?"

Leticia sighed, frustrated with the situation and frustrated that she was frustrated. Sharon took her hand again and squeezed gently. "Why don't you talk about what you two do, and I don't mean sex, okay? The other parts."

Leticia explained how she and Carter would get lunch together every day and he would buy her coffee in the morning—although now the two of them would go into the coffee shop together so she could chat with Hal while Carter bought their coffee. They had dinner together frequently, but not every day. Sometimes they'd get something and have it in the office while they finished going over the work for the day. One time, they'd actually ordered pizza and had it delivered to the museum, which had sent the security guards into fits of laughter.

Every spare moment, of course, they were having sex. Including in her office. And the men's restroom after hours. Any place without a video camera, in other words, because while the idea of having sex in front of the Chinese artwork was appealing, it wasn't worth it if a security guard caught them.

And the thing was, it was easy. She enjoyed Carter's energy. He was relaxed and sweet and he treated her better than any other man had.

"Let me guess, that's the problem," Sharon said.

Her affair with Ross and subsequent refusal to admit she was head over heels in love with him aside, Sharon had always been the responsible one. She wasn't the one who was having sex all the time. Hell, Ross had been her first one-night stand ever, if Leticia was remembering correctly. Leticia wasn't surprised that Sharon was able to read her like an illustrated novel.

She shrugged.

Sharon pressed on. "Leticia, is this about the whole relationship thing?"

"No?" Leticia answered. "Yes? Maybe?"

Sharon sighed. "I know that you haven't exactly had a chance to try out relationships, but do you really like this guy?"

"Of course I do," Leticia said, only realizing after she'd said it that she'd played her hand by responding so quickly and passionately.

Sharon, to her credit, didn't look too smug as she smiled at her. "It seems like this guy really respects you."

"Then why is he never available on weekends?" Leticia asked. "Why does he never spend the night? Why does he share so little about himself? I still know next to nothing about his previous relationships."

"That sounds like something you need to ask him about," Sharon replied.

"But what if that means he'll..."

"He's not going to reject you, Letty, Jesus."

"But what if he's with me because I'm easy?" Leticia asked. She was surprised to find that her voice sounded thick. "What if he's sticking around because I put out all the time and I'm good at sex—and I know I am, good at that, I mean, if nothing else. And because I'm his coworker and I'm right there and it's easy. What if that's why? What if the moment I start trying for more, or start pushing for anything, he writes me off?"

"I think that you should give him a little trust," Sharon replied. "Nobody is going to stick around and constantly be tested and judged. He seems to value you for who you are."

Leticia sighed. "I'm not—we're not dating, or anything. He's never said anything. I don't know why I'm even so worked up about this."

"You two have lunch together every day, he buys you coffee every morning, you have sex regularly and only with each other, and you go out to dinner a lot, most of the time where he insists that he pays." Sharon raised an eyebrow. "That sure sounds a hell of a lot like dating to me. I'd even go so far to say that," She faked a gasp, "You two are in an honest-to-God relationship!"

"You don't have to get sassy about it," Leticia grumbled, halfheartedly swiping her napkin at Sharon.

"You gave me so much crap about Ross," Sharon pointed out. "I think I can say that turnabout is fair play."

Leticia braced her elbows on the table and then put her head in her hands. "I just—I haven't done relationships, Shar. I don't know what I'm doing. I'm not used to this. I mean, it's not like I'm getting bored in the bedroom or anything."

Back when she'd been in college and a bit naïve about the whole sex thing, she'd thought that she would get bored sleeping with the same person over and over again. Sharon had contested that sex was better when you were in a relationship because there was more trust there, and because you two had time to really learn what the other person liked and didn't like, and so the sex got better as time went on, the way it couldn't with a one-night stand where it could be hit or miss.

At the time, Leticia had thought it was rather old-fashioned and had preferred to spend her time sleeping her way around, but now she was starting to understand what Sharon meant. The sex was good, and even better the more that they did it because, now, Carter knew that spot on her neck that would get her instantly wet. He knew that telling her to "spread your legs" made her feel like she'd been hooked up to a car battery.

So no, the sex wasn't the problem.

"It's just that he's so… he's nice, Sharon. He's really nice. And I keep waiting for the other shoe to drop."

"Where you find out that he's a serial killer who's going to take your skin?"

"You're getting a real kick out of this entire thing, aren't you?" Leticia replied.

Sharon held up her hands. "Sorry. I just—you gotta admit this is kind of amusing. You're Leticia. You've got the most sexual experience out of all of us. Combined. But you get into a relationship with a nice guy and you're running for the hills and looking for the boogie man?"

"I know, I know, I'm an idiot. You think I don't know that? But this is new territory for me. I don't have any idea what I'm doing."

Sharon shook her head. "That's the thing, sweetheart. None of us know what we're doing. You know me. I'd had some very serious relationships before Ross. Do you think I had any clue what I was doing when I was dating him? I was denying that I was dating him for most of it, for crying out loud. He practically had to propose to me before I'd admit to anyone that we were an official couple. Do you think Melanie's experience with men in any way prepares her for dating Debbie? Or that Debbie has any idea what she's doing with Melanie, who's a darling whom we love, but is also an anal-retentive control freak who has a panic spiral every five days?

"None of us know what we're doing here. We're all walking in blind, in every relationship, every time. We learn what we can, sure, but none of it is guaranteed. You don't know what life is going to throw at you. I would trust what you're seeing, which is that this is a good guy who cares about you. He obviously pays attention to your interests going by the kind of dates you've had, and he must be good in bed if you're risking awkwardness at the workplace for him. So what's the hold up?"

Leticia looked out the window for a moment. She knew that Sharon was right. Carter was amazing. She had never given much thought to what her dream man would look like. She hadn't had time to think about him. But if she had, she had a feeling that she would have imagined someone completely unlike Carter. She would have imagined someone fiery, like herself, someone passionate and talkative.

Carter was sweet and gentle, and a bit reticent. But he was also good at teasing her and was fucking amazing in the sack, and he paid attention to her and treated her like someone special. So no, she wouldn't have pictured anyone like Carter, and she would have been dead wrong because Carter was damn near perfect.

And it terrified her.

"He scares me," she admitted. "He's amazing. And that scares me."

"And neither of you have brought up this relationship thing, you said?" Sharon winced and then glared down at her stomach. "Behave, you," she said to the baby. Then she looked back at Leticia. "Maybe he's just as scared about this as you are. Why don't you talk to him? See what's up? You'll never get answers until you ask, right?"

"I suppose so."

"And if it's a good outcome, you can have enthusiastic monkey sex that you will tell me all about in the morning." Sharon smiled beatifi-cally up at their waiter, who had arrived with their food (and Sharon's triple side order of bacon) just at that moment, which caused Leticia to turn an alarming shade of pink.

Ross really must be rubbing off on her, Leticia thought, if Sharon was unfazed by the waiter overhearing her say the phrase 'enthusiastic monkey sex'.

"As I was saying, you're going to tell me all about it if it's a good outcome, and you're going to come over right away and cry with me and eat ice cream if it's bad." Sharon started tucking into her meal. "I'll make sure Ross is out of the way, if he isn't already out on a call, and we'll have a good old-fashioned girls' night in, just like when we were living together."

Leticia nodded. "All right. Thanks for helping me keep my head on straight, and all that."

"Hey, you helped me when it looked like my boyfriend was going to get fired for sleeping with me because he had the abusive ex from hell," Sharon pointed out. "It's only fair. We're friends, Leticia. It's what we do. Now promise that you'll keep me updated, okay?"

"Okay." Leticia nodded. "We're going out tonight, this time to a painting class."

"Oh my God, a painting class. You two are totally a couple, whether you admit it or not." Sharon made a gagging noise and Leticia snorted.

"Like you've got any leg to stand on. If you and Ross get any cuter, I think that Jonas is going to actually vomit at the next get-together." Leticia made a face.

"Once upon a time, you would have been threatening that you would be the one vomiting." Sharon shook her head in mock sadness. "Love has changed you, Letty. It really has."

"Oh, shut up."

"Now, c'mon." Sharon grinned wickedly. "Tell me all about this crazy good sex you've apparently been having and haven't been telling me about, you traitor."

The rest of the lunch passed in laughter, Leticia regaling Sharon about her sexual exploits with Carter, which she was more than happy to tell someone about. She'd been keeping it quiet, which she knew was unusual for her. Perhaps that should have been a sign that this guy was different and that she should have been talking to Sharon about it sooner. Oh, well.

Afterwards, Leticia made sure that Sharon got back to her car safely and then drove back to work. She'd done her best to cram all of her work into the morning so that she could take her time with Sharon, but she still faced a daunting mountain when she got back.

"Friday, thank God," Carter pointed out, strolling into her office almost as soon as she sat down. "Hey, could you have a word with Tom? He's been going off-script on the tours again apparently and, I don't mind his embellishments about certain artists' affairs, but his language is offending a few people, apparently."

Leticia held in a sigh. "Yeah, I'll talk to him on Monday. I've got to get this paperwork finished."

Carter looked at her for a moment, then walked over and around to stand at the back of her desk chair and put his hands on her shoulders. "Just relax," he told her, when Leticia tensed up to start protesting.

She relaxed as best she could, letting Carter start massaging her. She really didn't have time for this—she'd already wasted, enough time today with Sharon even though that was important life stuff, and she had to get this all done before their date that evening—but she couldn't resist. Not when Carter was digging his thumbs expertly right into her sore muscles and slowly working all of the knots out of her body.

Leticia let her head fall forward and groaned in relaxed pleasure. "Where the hell did you get so good at this?"

"My—someone I knew taught me."

There it was, one of those little pauses. There weren't too many of them, but there were enough to make Leticia suspicious. It wasn't that she thought that Carter was a criminal or a cheater or anything. She just knew that there were things in his life, specifically in his past, that he wasn't yet comfortable telling her about. That made her nervous.

What if he thought that she wasn't worthy of hearing those things? What if he didn't trust her enough?

She did her best to breathe and stay calm. This would never resolve itself until she just talked to him, like a normal adult. She could do that. She was a normal adult. Most of the time.

"I hope that helps," Carter said. He gave her a soft, quick kiss on the side of her neck and then stepped back.

"I feel like the bones in my body have turned to jelly," Leticia admitted. "And hey, I might ask you for one every day. Because I am greedy."

Carter laughed. "Finish up your paperwork. We have reservations."

"So bossy. I thought I was the one in charge around here."

"We all like to give you that delusion," Carter replied, because he might be private but he was also a cheeky asshole who liked to tease her and knew that she liked the teasing, dammit, because she was a weak, weak woman. "I'll leave you alone to work now. See you in a few hours?"

"You bet."

So this was the routine that they'd fallen into, Leticia realized. It was a routine... They had one of those. They would work and Carter would come in and distract her for a short bit to keep them from going crazy, and they'd have lunch together, and then Friday they went out somewhere that Carter picked out for them and it was always awesome...

Oh my God, she thought. Sharon was right. We've totally become a couple when I wasn't looking.

Shit.

She tried not to have a panic attack all through the rest of the work day, and all through their way to dinner, and all through dinner itself. Sharon was the one who had panic attacks, she reminded herself. She, Leticia, was the cool one who was never fazed by anything.

"So—I'm sorry, I don't mean to pry or insult you or anything. But I just don't understand how you managed to avoid having a serious relationship all these years."

Carter was speaking, Leticia realized. She had completely lost track of the conversation.

"I wasn't really into relationships in high school," she admitted. "Or a while after that. I thought that it would be boring."

She was pretty sure that this topic coming up while she was so nervous about the whole relationships thing was a sign that the universe hated her.

"I just find that funny, because I always wanted to be with someone." Carter gave a self-deprecating shrug. "I always had a girlfriend. I think it was a bit of a problem, actually. I couldn't be single."

"You managed to be single pretty well until you met me," Leticia pointed out.

"Yes, well…" Carter cleared his throat. "That's because I was—"

He took a deep breath, as though steeling himself. "I was in mourning."

"Mourning?" Leticia was pretty sure that both of Carter's parents were still alive, the way he talked about them in the present tense and all.

Carter swallowed and nodded. "My wife. Olivia. I was—I was married."

Leticia felt as though she couldn't breathe. She remembered how scared she'd been during Sharon's accident—helpless to do anything, stuck on the phone as her friend lost consciousness, not knowing if Sharon was okay or the extent of the damage as she frantically called 9-1-1. She couldn't even begin to image what that must be like with someone you'd chosen to spend the rest of your life with. She couldn't imagine what it felt like when the person was actually gone.

"I'm so sorry," she blurted out genuinely, knowing the words were inadequate. She reached out and took Carter's hand. He squeezed hers gently, gratefully.

"It's okay. I mean, it's not okay, of course, but there's no reason for you to be sorry. If that makes any sense. We met in college, in one of my classes. She was the brightest person in the room. I'd broken up with my latest high school girlfriend when we went off to different colleges and I had promised myself that, this time, it would be different. This time I was at college. I'd stay single for a while, learn about myself, really explore who I was and all of that."

Carter gave a small, self-deprecating laugh. "Look how well that turned out. I fell in love with her freshman year and we dated all through college."

"That sounds so sweet," Leticia said. "What did she do? What was she like?"

"She was kind of like you, not afraid to speak her mind," Carter admitted. "She was an architecture student, so we had some overlapping classes and were both part of the art department, in different capacities.

"Liv—that's what I called her—she brought out the best in me. And when... well, it was a blood disease. I won't go into details, but in runs in both sides of her family. When it's just one side, it's fairly dormant or manageable or something like that, I don't quite remember. But when you've got both sides... Something about the genes... But she had it from both sides and it—we had some time, but it was scary how rapidly her body just... shut down."

Carter shook himself a little. "I'm sorry. I haven't really talked to anyone about it. My friends all know, of course. And my parents. But it's different. When you talk to someone who knows versus someone who doesn't. When they know, you feel kind of—redundant, I suppose, is the word. But you don't know about any of it, and you didn't know her, and that's kind of... Freeing, I guess, to talk to you about it."

"I hope that I can be supportive," Leticia replied. She felt like an idiot. What was she supposed to say? What was she supposed to do? She had no idea.

"It just feels good to tell you about it," Carter admitted. "I wasn't sure how to bring it up, but the longer that went on the worse I felt about it. It's going to affect our relationship, after all."

Ah, so they were in a relationship, Leticia wanted to say, but she kept it to herself. She didn't think that right at that moment was a good time to bring up their relationship status.

"I have to be honest, I'm not sure what to say or do here," Leticia told him. "But I want to support you. I've never experienced anything like that. I can't even imagine... But I want to be respectful of what you went through, so if there's anything in particular you need me to do, you just let me know."

"Just keep doing what you're doing," Carter said, smiling at her. "You've been really great so far. And I'm sorry that I've been tight-lipped about this. It's hard, you know? To let someone else in afterwards. How do you even begin to explain? I mean, half the time people think that you're supposed to be sad all the time, and in a way, you are, but in a way, you're also not."

"I suppose that makes sense," Leticia replied. "I know this isn't the same thing but my grandmother died my second year of college. That was the first time that Sharon met my extended family, actually, she was really awesome and flew down with me to go to the funeral. I just —you know how family can be awesome but also overwhelming? Sharon helped with the overwhelming part.

"But when I got back to school, everyone who knew what had happened acted as though I was supposed to be crying all the time. Nobody who'd actually lost a grandparent thought that. But the people who hadn't lost a grandparent did. They didn't understand how I could be smiling and okay all the time. And there were times when I really wasn't okay, but I didn't let everyone see it. It was private."

"Exactly." Carter nodded. "Right. It's a different sort of grief, just like every kind of grief is different. But you don't want to just talk about the grief. You want to find a way to be normal again. The problem is...normal used to include them. It used to include Olivia, for me. Finding that new normal is important. And after a while, that new normal started to include the idea of dating again, since I do want that person in my life."

"I'm..." Leticia paused, then laughed. "I sound like I'm accepting an award or something. I'm honored that you chose me to be that person, at least for now."

Carter smiled at her. "You are definitely that person right now."

Leticia could feel herself blushing and quickly looked down at her plate.

"So what do your parents do?" Carter asked. He gave her a watery smile and Leticia understood that he wanted her to change the subject. She squeezed his hand once and then let go, settling back into her chair. If he needed them to change the subject, that was fine by her.

"My mom's a teacher," she explained, "And my dad's a sewage guy. Mom's job pays crap but you actually get good benefits when you work for a sewage plant. It's physical labor and not everyone wants to do it and the union's still strong, so, Dad was able to take care of us. We didn't live in the best areas but we were able to go to college, something our relatives kept telling my parents they weren't sure we could pull off."

"That's really great," Carter said. Leticia gave him a mental point for not making a joke about her dad's profession. If she had to hear one more off-color joke about it from someone, she was not going to be responsible for her actions.

"What about your parents?" She asked. "I know you said that your mom had time to volunteer at the local art museum."

"Oh, they're both dentists." Carter grimaced. "The most boring job in the world, if you'd asked me while I was growing up. That was how they met, actually, at some convention or something. Mom had her own practice but, after she got pregnant with me, she opted to be a stay-at-home mom and she started doing volunteer work while I was at school. She was one of those people that had always wanted kids, you know?"

"I've never understood that," Leticia admitted. "I mean, kids are fine, but I've never felt especially connected to them. And I kind of have this fear of being pregnant. My mom had a really difficult pregnancy, both with me and with my twin brothers, and I've got the same body shape as she does. I fear that I'll have the same issues, y'know?"

"What about adoption?" Carter suggested.

"I've thought about it, but I think I just don't want kids in general. I never know how to act around them." Leticia made a face. "I'm sorry, it's not that I don't like kids. People tend to take that as an attack on all children and it's not, I'm just—most people seem to know instinctively what to do with babies and children and I just, I just don't. I don't know."

"That's all right," Carter replied, but Leticia thought she heard an odd note in his voice. "It doesn't come to everyone naturally."

"Right." Leticia wanted desperately to change the subject. Talking about kids was far too serious a subject for how early they were in their relationship. Since, apparently, they were in a relationship. "You mentioned that you met Olivia in college. Where did you go?"

After that, the topics got back onto safer ground. They swapped college stories and discussed art, although they had an unspoken agreement not to talk about work specifically while they were out for dinner. Work was for their lunches or at the museum.

Leticia thought that the night went well for the most part, but something about Carter seemed off to her. She couldn't quite put her finger on it. Everything had been going fine and she couldn't think of anything she'd said that would make him feel hurt or offended.

Was it talking about his dead wife, Olivia? Had that made him realize that Leticia couldn't measure up to her? Or had she reacted inappropriately in some way? She didn't think that she had, but, what did she know?

She knew for certain that something was wrong when they reached the end of the night. Normally this was the part when Carter would start to turn on the sex appeal. Around dessert, he'd do something—let her see him looking her over, or give her a stare that spoke volumes of intimacy, and she would respond with something blatantly sexual. Afterwards, they'd head back to her place.

One time, they actually hadn't waited to get back to her place and had sex in the car. Leticia shivered at the memory.

But Carter seemed oddly...closed off. She'd noticed that Carter was generally reserved.. For how sweet he was, he wasn't one to really volunteer a ton of information. She still didn't know a whole lot about his friends, for instance, even though they'd been the people he'd been out with when they'd first met.

This wasn't his usual reserved behavior, however. It was like she could see the "Closed for Business" sign hanging around his neck.

She tried anyway, once the bill was paid and they were getting up to go. Carter helped her into her coat and they started to make their way out of the restaurant. Everything seemed to be how it normally was, at least on the surface.

"Would you like to come back to my place tonight?" Leticia asked. She felt more tentative than usual but tried to be her usual coy, flirty self.

"I can't," Carter told her. "I have to get back. Early night and all that."

Leticia actually didn't know what 'all that' meant because he never told her. And while Carter never stayed the night, he hadn't had to turn in quite this early before. Sharon had suggested at some point during their lunch that his not staying the night could have nothing to do with her—he could have bad insomnia, for instance—but this definitely felt like she was being placed at arm's length.

"Okay then," she said, trying not to let her disappointment show in her face or her voice. She didn't want Carter feeling sorry for her.

She wanted to write it off as just sex, but that wasn't it. Sometimes people just didn't want to have sex, that was true, even men. But this— this didn't feel like that. It felt like she'd messed up at some point and she couldn't figure out why and so she couldn't fix it.

The drive back to her apartment was silent. Leticia didn't know what to say to make things less uncomfortable. She didn't even know if things were as uncomfortable as she was imagining them to be. Carter seemed lost in his own thoughts.

The only time that things got a little back to normal was the moment when he dropped her off. "Have a good weekend," he told her, pulling her in for a quick kiss. "I'll see you Monday."

That, at least, was normal—telling her to have a good weekend and saying he'd see her on Monday. Even the quick kiss was normal. Leticia clung to it and prayed that it meant she hadn't messed things up too badly, whatever it was.

"Yeah, you have a good weekend, too," she told him.

The moment he pulled away, she called Sharon.

"And!?" Sharon demanded.

Leticia told her what had happened. "And I don't know how I messed up!" She finished. "Clearly I said something wrong. Was I disrespectful about his wife? Did talking about her make him realize that he wasn't ready to move on from her? Did he realize we were moving too fast for him? Did he—"

"Breathe, Letty, before you pass out," Sharon replied. "Just breathe with me for a moment, okay? Nothing is going to get better if you panic."

"I'm supposed to be the one helping you through panic attacks," Leticia mourned, collapsing onto her couch. "I'm the calm, fun one. When did things switch?"

"When you decided to try something that's scary for you," Sharon replied. "It's okay to be nervous about all of this. You know that."

"Knowing it intellectually and experiencing it are two very different things," Leticia pointed out.

"All right, fair. But remember, this is going to be okay, all right? Whatever it is, it'll turn out okay. I mean, I turned out pretty okay, didn't I?"

Leticia laughed despite herself. "Fair point."

"Excellent." She could sense Sharon's smile through the phone. "Now, did you talk with him about this? Did you ask him if you'd done anything wrong?"

"No." Leticia groaned. "I'm a coward, Sharon, when are you going to realize this?"

"You are not a coward. You're just not used to this. This was my forte, remember? I was the one who did all those long relationships. You were so good at one-night stands. Remember when I slept with Ross and flipped out? This is just the reverse."

"I suppose."

"Now, listen to your wise relationship guru," Sharon continued. "You need to talk to him about this. Even if it turns out to just be a little thing. Or maybe it's something that you misunderstood, you know, maybe you were projecting onto him. We do that sometimes when we're scared about something. We think that the other person is judging us or something like that when they're not, it's just us judging ourselves. Be gentle on yourself, okay? And talk to him."

"What do I even say?" Leticia asked.

"You say that you hope this isn't weird, but you were getting an odd vibe from him last night after you talked about his wife. You want to be sure that you didn't say or do anything to make him uncomfortable. If he says it's nothing like that, or that you didn't do anything, then tell him that if there's anything about this relationship that he feels needs to change—like if he needs to take a step back or something—you're okay with that."

Leticia nodded, trying to remember all of that. "You make it all seem so logical and simple."

"It is when you're the one on the outside. Just breathe and remember that whatever this is, you can fix it through calm communication, okay sweetheart?"

"Okay." Leticia sighed. "I think he's becoming really important to me, Shar. That kind of scares me. No, it really freaks me out!!"

"It always scares us," Sharon replied. "It scares me when I make new friends, actually. Do you remember when I was panicking because I had realized that Debbie was a part of our usual schedule senior year? She'd get lunch with us every day and stuff?"

Leticia smiled. "Yeah, and I asked you what the problem was, and you said that you were scared about how much you cared about her."

"Exactly. Her friendship was starting to really mean something to me, and that scared me because friends can hurt you just as much as lovers do. People just tend to forget that, I think. So this is something that we're all experiencing, hon. It's scary because you care, but it's the only way we can do it."

"Careful there. That almost sounded profound."

"I do have my moments." Sharon sighed fondly. "Now go to sleep. Get some rest. Watch a movie or eat some ice cream if that'll help you to relax. Then tomorrow morning you can call him and ask what was up, okay?"

"Okay." Leticia sighed. "Okay, I will. I'll do that."

"Great. I love you."

"Love you, too."

She hung up but stayed flopped on the couch for a moment.

Right. Get some rest and call Carter in the morning. Try not to freak out about anything in the meantime. Communicate clearly and calmly. It probably wasn't as big of a deal as she was making it seem, so—just stay calm. Don't freak out.

Easier said than done.

CHAPTER 11

$\mathcal{L}$eticia waited until around ten o'clock to call Carter. She figured that since he was a morning person he might be up earlier, but she didn't know for certain. The way that he always talked about having an early morning on Saturday, he might have some kind of class or family thing that he wasn't back from yet.

Besides, she'd been raised by parents who taught her that you didn't call anyone after nine o'clock at night or before nine o'clock in the morning. That rule had definitely become lax over the years when it came to her friends. With Sharon, that rule didn't even exist. They'd called each other at all hours of the day—hell, when Sharon was leaving Ross's place after that first night they were together, she'd called Leticia at two in the morning.

Luckily Leticia had been out at a club at the time and partying hard, but still.

She hadn't been to any clubs since dating Carter, actually. She hadn't needed to. Why would she when she was already tired after spending a full night with him on Fridays? Then, on Saturdays, she was usually with one of her friends instead, like out at a bar with Jonas or over helping Sharon make dinner. And why go out on a Sunday night when she had work early Monday morning? That was a mistake she'd made her first year out of college and not one she was going to repeat.

But it scared her all over again—how much her schedule had changed because of Carter and how she hadn't even realized it until now. It made her wonder what other ways she might have come to depend on him, ways she wouldn't notice until it was too late and she was too far gone.

That nervousness was probably why she'd gotten up at eight o'clock and then spent two hours trying desperately to distract herself while waiting for an appropriate time to call him.

She'd run the laundry, vacuumed, done the dishes, and watched a bunch of HGTV. She was convinced that the couples hunting for houses were all just a little bit insane, yet the shows were strangely addicting.

Then ten o'clock had come. No more excuses.

Leticia steeled herself and dialed Carter's number. She'd had it in her phone for ages, but she'd had little reason to use it other than the occasional text during work. Those texts had often made her smile, especially when one of them was stuck in a meeting. This was the first time she'd actually called him.

The phone rang a couple of times and was then picked up—but not by Carter.

"Hello?"

The speaker was a girl. A very young girl, judging by the voice.

"Hi, who is this?" Leticia asked. Maybe Carter had lost his phone or something?

"I'm Molly," answered the girl. "Who are you?"

"I'm—my name is Leticia. Is Carter around?" Leticia was scrambling for answers. Who was this girl? Why did she have Carter's phone? Did he have family in town—a niece or something—and he'd failed to mention it?

Or, maybe he hadn't wanted to mention it, the traitorous part of her brain supplied.

"Oh, yeah, Daddy's in the shower," Molly replied.

Leticia felt like her stomach had suddenly disappeared.

"He's—what?"

"Daddy's in the shower," Molly repeated. "Sorry about that. Would you like me to take a message?"

"No, it's okay," Leticia said. She had to sit down, right now. She did so, collapsing onto her couch again. What the hell? "I'm his boss, from work at the museum—"

Molly interrupted before Leticia could continue. "Oh, right! You work with him now! I remember he told me that his boss was a woman. I think that's really great, you're in charge of an entire museum. Do you like it?"

Leticia swallowed hard. "Um, yeah. I like it a lot."

"I love art," Molly said. "Daddy's taught me all about it. I mean, not all about it, I don't know everything, but a lot. I love it. I do art, too. What's your favorite painting?"

Leticia definitely could not handle this at the moment. Not while it felt like her entire world was off-kilter and spinning. "That's hard to say. Listen, Molly, I hate to cut our conversation short, but I have to go, okay?"

"Oh, but I can just talk to you until Daddy gets out," Molly replied. "He'll be finished soon."

She definitely couldn't talk to Carter about this right now. Hell no. She might throw up if she had to have this conversation—and over the phone, of all things. It was better than, say, discussing it over email, but still. She wasn't going to talk about something like this when she couldn't see Carter's face or when he could easily hang up on her if he got pissed off.

"I wish I could," she replied, "But I've got a meeting."

"On a Saturday?" Molly asked. "That's not fair. Weekends are for fun things. You should be out having fun."

Leticia smiled a little in spite of herself. "Yeah, kid, that's always been my philosophy. But I really do have to go, so how about you just have a good day for me, okay?"

"Do you want me to tell Daddy anything for you? Preserving art is very important."

That was...kind of adorable of her to say. Molly sounded incredibly solemn about it. She sounded the way Leticia felt inside when she talked about taking care of art and making sure it was properly preserved.

"No, it was just a little thing. I shouldn't have bothered him." Leticia found herself seriously starting to feel sick. Her throat felt tight and her eyes itched—crap. "Have a good day."

"You too, Leticia!" Molly replied brightly.

Leticia ended the call and stared at the phone in her hand.

What the hell, what the hell, *what the hell?*

Carter had a child?

An older child, too. Not a baby or a toddler. A child who was old enough to talk a bit about art and hold an intelligent conversation and answer the phone on her own. At least five. Maybe even as old as nine? Leticia wasn't good at gaging the age of kids, especially when she couldn't see what they looked like. Little hellions refused to grow uniformly, so she'd see a twelve-year-old that looked like a seven-year-old and then a five-year-old that looked like an eight-year-old.

As if kids weren't confusing enough already.

Leticia wondered if she should call Sharon and tell her about this. But hadn't she bothered her friend enough? Sharon was her best friend, sure, but Sharon was pregnant and trying to hand over the reins for maternity leave and she had a husband whose work schedule was erratic at best. She didn't deserve to listen to Leticia's third freak-out in a row.

No. Obviously this was why Carter had become distant last night. It hadn't been while they were talking about Olivia, his wife. It had been while they were talking about kids, afterwards. When Leticia had said that she didn't want to have kids and she'd never been very good with them. That had been when Carter had shut down on her. He'd started writing her off, she realized. He'd put the brakes on the idea of 'them'.

He was probably already thinking of ways to ease himself out of the relationship, Leticia thought bitterly. Cut and run, so to speak.

But could she blame him? She'd said that she didn't like children. She hadn't been coy about that. Leticia could only cover her face and groan. God, she felt sick. She must have sounded like a complete asshole last night.

At least she hadn't said that she hated kids. And she didn't. Hate kids, that is. But she'd said that she didn't want any and that she wasn't any good with them—and that was just as bad as hating them, wasn't it? At least in the eyes of a parent?

But on the other hand—why hadn't Carter told her right away that he had a kid? Wasn't that the first thing that parents did, tell you all about their children? Okay, so fair enough, he wouldn't mention it when he was at a club and they were clearly about to have sex. That wasn't really a good opportunity to get to know one another.

As his boss, though, as coworkers, surely he would have said something. Why hadn't he? Didn't he want to talk about his daughter? Or had Leticia had a huge neon *I hate kids* sign over her head this entire time and he'd suspected as much and so he hadn't said anything?

Damn, she was talking herself in circles. She just needed to be distracted. She needed—she needed something.

She needed to go out and dance to the bang bang slide of the club bass.

Carter obviously wasn't going to continue this relationship. He'd already started pulling away last night, and Leticia couldn't expect him to continue to date someone when he had a kid at home. Hell, he plainly hadn't trusted her with the knowledge of his daughter even before she'd said that she wasn't good with kids.

She should cut her losses while she could. Carter was going to move on—well, so could she. They could just be friendly coworkers, nothing more. And all of that would start with her. She could be the big girl here. She could step away and let him know that it was okay, that he didn't owe her anything.

He didn't want to owe her anything, if he hadn't told her about his daughter. If he'd thought this relationship was serious in any way, then he would have told her about Molly. But he hadn't. So…

Clearly Leticia had been the one who'd gotten in over her head, here.

That hurt. It hurt more than she expected it to. God, no wonder Jonas was so cranky after a break-up.

But, as previously stated, she was a big girl. She could handle this.

First, ice cream. And tonight?

She was hitting the clubs like there was no tomorrow.

CHAPTER 12

*C*arter had to admit that he needed to take the weekend to think about things.

When Leticia had been so supportive about Olivia, he'd been elated. All right, so maybe elated wasn't the right word to use. But it had been easier than he'd expected to talk to Leticia about it. She'd listened, really listened, and she hadn't said all those trite things that other people had said like, "You poor man," or "Well, I'm sure she's in a better place."

She'd admitted that she hadn't ever experienced anything like that but had told him she was sorry it had happened. There, nice and simple. He had never understood why people felt the need to say more. It was like most people were uncomfortable with grief, so they talked too much in order to try and fight their way through the discomfort.

And thank God she hadn't said anything like, "But you hide it so well! I had no idea! That's so brave of you."

Various people had told him that over the years. It had always pissed him off. How was he supposed to look? Was he supposed to be wearing black and weeping all the time? It was like people thought that if a tragedy struck you, you were going to wear it on your sleeve.

That somehow everyone around you would be able to tell, like you had a black eye or something.

But Leticia had been great. She'd been quietly supportive and listened to him as he talked about it. She hadn't pried for more information, either, which was really nice. Some people thought that him telling them about Olivia meant he was inviting them to ask all about her, when that wasn't it at all. He just wanted them to know that it was a thing, like the fact that he worked in a museum. It and she were a part of him.

It was all going swimmingly and he was genuinely excited. Leticia had taken the news about Olivia well. That meant, for one thing, that he could mention her now, bring her up in casual conversation.

It would be nice, he had thought. Leticia hadn't known Olivia when she was alive and so he could freely share memories of her without Leticia jumping in or saying, "I know" or anything like that. He could share the memory just as it was.

Then the subject of kids had come up.

He hadn't even meant for the conversation to swing that way. While Leticia's acceptance of Olivia meant that he was hopeful she was going to be accepting of Molly, a dead wife did not equal a very alive and demanding child. Not that Molly was demanding but—all children demanded a lot of time and attention, just by nature of being children.

With Olivia out of the way, he'd figured that he'd bring Molly up sometime in the next couple of weeks. He'd get Leticia used to the idea of Olivia having been in his life, of having her mentioned. Then he'd feel out how Leticia was with kids.

Then he'd made that throwaway comment about his mom and it had all gone to hell.

Okay, so maybe 'hell' was a bit of an exaggeration. But it hadn't gone the way he had wanted it to, not at all. It was like someone had thrown a bucket of ice water in his face.

Leticia didn't like kids. She didn't want kids. She didn't get along well with kids—or rather, she didn't know how to handle them. It wasn't outright telling him that she hated kids, so that was a silver lining. But how could he possibly be in a relationship with someone who wouldn't accept Molly?

Not that he was sure that Leticia wouldn't accept Molly. Most people he'd met who weren't all that into kids generally struggled with babies and toddlers. Perhaps it was the same way with Leticia? Maybe an older child like Molly, especially one as mature as Molly was, would be something Leticia would be more willing to accept.

He wasn't sure, though, and that was the problem. Could he continue this relationship based on a 'maybe'?

It had taken him all weekend to think about it. Molly could tell that he was preoccupied and so she mostly left him alone. She did her homework and did her drawing, but she didn't pester him to play chess with her or anything. Carter appreciated it. He just sat with a book idly in his lap, reading the same page ten times until he gave up and just watched Molly as she drew or ran around the backyard playing pirate.

By the time Monday arrived, he had a plan. He would introduce Leticia to Molly that afternoon. Not literally, of course. Not in person. He'd just tell her about Molly while they were at lunch. That would get it all out in the open. He'd tell Leticia that she could have a few days to think about it, but he'd like her to meet Molly on Friday, when they had their usual date night. It wouldn't even be a date, he would just arrange for Molly to stop by the museum close to closing and Leticia could meet Molly in her capacity as Daddy's boss. Then, if they hit it off, he and Leticia could keep dating and he'd slowly introduce her and Molly to one another.

If she and Molly didn't hit it off, well, at least he'd have his answer right away. And if Leticia backed off immediately when he brought it up at lunch, he'd have his answer then as well.

And he would let her go, even if the idea of breaking things off with her pained him more than he wanted to really admit to himself.

When he arrived at the coffee shop, however, Leticia wasn't there.

"Hey, Hal," he said, entering the shop. Hal looked up from where she was cleaning the espresso machine. "Any sign of Leticia?"

"No, she hasn't been by." Hal furrowed her brow questioningly.

"She usually meets you, so I figured she'd be here with you. She hasn't texted you or anything?"

He double-checked his phone, just in case. "Nope."

"Maybe she's running late."

"Maybe."

Hal shrugged and went back to doing her job. Carter waited. And waited. And waited.

Eventually he had to resign himself to the fact that for whatever reason, Leticia wasn't coming this morning. Maybe she was running late enough that she couldn't stop by before she had to be at the museum? She'd never been late before but he knew Leticia wasn't a morning person. There was bound to be a morning where she couldn't drag herself out of bed until the last minute.

When he reached the museum, he found that Leticia was already there. He tried not to think anything of it—until he saw that in her hand was a to-go coffee cup. From another coffee shop.

It was a chain coffee shop too, which didn't make sense, because they'd had a passionate discussion at lunch where Leticia had declared herself a snob and said she never went to chain coffee shops and stayed loyal to the local, individually-owned places.

Things got more concerning when he walked up to her. He put a smile on, ready to pull her in and kiss her hello. He knew that he had to make up for Friday night. He'd been shaken and he'd sort of pulled back into himself—and he'd said no to sex for the first time. She had to be wondering what was going on and he'd need to reassure her.

But when he reached out to wrap an arm around her waist and pull her into him, Leticia took a step back. She gave him a huge smile, though, which confused him. "Morning!" She said brightly. "I put some paperwork on your desk, I was hoping that you could give it a double-check for me? I'm going to be in meetings for most of the day, so don't worry if you don't see me much, just shoot me an email if you have any questions. You know what else to do."

"Uh…" Carter wasn't sure what to do with this new Leticia. There wasn't a single hint of flirtation or innuendo or intimacy about her. That was completely unlike the Leticia he knew.

Actually, it was a little like the way Leticia had been the very first day, when they'd each been startled by the fact that they'd accidentally slept with their new coworker. But this was—this was odd.

"Okay," he said, for a lack of anything better to say. "I'll get on that. Thanks."

"Thanks!" Leticia said before turning smartly on her heel to walk off down the hallway.

So, maybe she was having an off day or something? Carter hadn't known how to approach the subject, so he had just let it slide. He'd kind of bailed on her on Friday, so he figured she deserved a weird day, too.

He tried not to take it personally when she told him that she had a lunch meeting and couldn't join him at their usual Thai place.

That had been Monday. Tuesday, she wasn't in front of the coffee shop again.

"She hasn't been by?" He asked Hal.

Hal shook her head. The girl looked a little concerned, actually. Carter remembered that Leticia had actually been frequenting this coffee shop far longer than he had. In fact, he'd started coming to this coffee shop because of Leticia.

"Has she ever not come by before?" He asked.

Hal thought for a moment. "Very, very rarely," she said. "But those would usually be days when she didn't have work for some reason. Otherwise, she's always here. And two days in a row? Nah. She'll even stop by on public holidays because, even if the museum's closed, she's still working on something in the office."

Carter nodded. "Thanks, Hal."

Hal nodded, still looking a bit worried.

When he went to the museum, Leticia was there, a generic chain brand coffee in hand. She was already in her office this time, going over something on her computer.

"Oh, good, you're here," she said cheerfully. When he started to get close to the desk she just thrust a file into his hand. "If you could take care of this for me, I'd really appreciate it. I have a lunch meeting today but, otherwise, I'm pretty free. So if you need anything, just let me know."

"What if I'd like a meeting?" Carter asked, infusing his voice with innuendo. "Say, in my office? In an hour?"

Leticia just blinked at him. "Is there something about the latest exhibit I need to know about? Did the artist change where he wanted to put the centerpiece?"

Carter felt wrong footed. "Um—no, I meant..." He stopped. He wasn't sure how to say *I meant we should have sex in my office* without it sounding incredibly crass. "Never mind."

"Okay." Leticia smiled at him, but it was a lighthearted, professional smile. It was nothing like the way she'd been smiling at him before.

Then she went right back to her work, as if he wasn't even there.

The rest of the week had gone the same way. Leticia treated him with friendliness, but she kept a distinct distance between the two of them. She somehow managed to have a lunch meeting every day. She was never there for her coffee.

That last part pissed him off a bit, actually. Poor Hal was worried.

"Is something wrong?" She asked on the third morning. "Is she sick? Does she seem unwell? Is her family okay?"

Carter had been forced to tell her that no, nothing seemed to be wrong with Leticia, she just wasn't getting her coffee from their coffee place anymore.

"You did something, didn't you?" Hal asked—rather accusingly, Carter thought. "What the hell did you do, Carter? She's my favorite customer. Tell her you won't come back and I'll take her. She should claim me in the divorce."

Carter didn't even know how to begin to respond to that sentence and, frankly, he didn't want to. He just left Hal to her mutterings.

Whenever he tried to talk to her about it, Leticia brushed him off.

"Do you have a second?" Carter asked on Wednesday.

"What's it about?" Leticia replied.

"It's about..." He gestured between the two of them.

Leticia looked uncomprehending. "Unless it's about the art, I really have to make a phone call, so can it wait?"

"Sure."

He'd tried later in the afternoon on the same day. "Why aren't you having lunch with me anymore?"

"Oh, I'm sorry, I just realized that it saved me time if I had meetings during lunch. Saved me having to take time out of the rest of my workday to deal with those divas and bores, you know?"

Then again, on Thursday: "I think that we need to talk." Delivered in his most serious voice possible, of course.

"I'm really sorry, but I've got to run and check on the installation. Oh, and could you be a pal and look at this one contract for me? I think the guy's asking for too much but I'd like a second opinion before I unleash the dragon on him. Thanks!"

Finally, Carter had to resign himself to the fact that whatever it was, Leticia just didn't want to talk to him about it.

Why had she suddenly stopped treating him like they were a couple? Could it have been his mention of Olivia? She'd seemed perfectly okay with it at the time. Had something about it scared her off and she'd just done a good job of hiding it?

He'd thought that they were embarking on something serious. They spent two thirds of their time together, after all, getting coffee before work and then work itself and lunch during work and then dinner at least three times a week, including official dates on Fridays. Carter supposed that he'd been the only one thinking of it that way, if Leticia could turn on a dime like this.

Still, he couldn't help but wonder what had made her behave like this. It had to have been something that he said or did that Friday, but what?

And why was it upsetting him so much?

CHAPTER 13

*L*eticia sank onto the couch next to Tom. At least he and Jonas were still single along with her, she thought to herself glumly. The three of them could counteract the two happy couples.

"How was your week?" She asked him.

Over in the kitchen, Sharon and Jonas were complaining about the latest episode of some reality television show or other. Leticia hadn't bothered to figure out what. Debbie was sitting on the chair, reading some amusing internet story out loud to Ross and Melanie.

"It was fine. Sold two paintings, which was great. One of the guys is from New York, talked about getting me to be one of the artists at this gallery showing."

"That's great!" Leticia beamed at him. "I told you, people are starting to notice your work."

Tom would never be an internationally-known artist, but he was building himself a very respectable following on the Eastern seaboard. Leticia had high hopes for him.

"How about your week?" Tom asked. "Something's on your mind."

Leticia didn't even bother trying to hide it. "Am I that obvious?"

"Normally you're the life of the party," Tom replied. "Today you've hardly said a word."

"Can't a girl have a quiet day?"

"Sure, if the girl's quiet days weren't always the days that she had some major issue she was trying to work through."

"It's not a major issue." Leticia huffed. "It's kind of ridiculous, actually."

"What's ridiculous?" Sharon asked, walking over just in time to hear the last bit.

"Something's got our girl down in the dumps," Tom said.

"Way to rat me out," Leticia said, but she laid her head on Tom's shoulder. Tom was arguably the most soft-spoken of the group. Even Sharon could be prone to sassiness and energy. Tom was the calm eye in the middle of the storm that was their friend group.

Tom patted her leg kindly. "You know you need to talk about it. That's what we're here for."

"Ugh, must you be right all the time?"

"What is it?" Debbie asked, catching on that something was happening. "Did something crazy happen at the club?"

Leticia made a face. She'd gone to the club that Saturday after talking to Carter's daughter, but it hadn't felt right. The music was fun, still, and she enjoyed dancing, but she'd wished the whole time that she had a specific partner to dance with, someone she'd come to club with who would dance with her throughout the night. She hadn't wanted to pick anyone up and she hadn't even felt like drinking very much.

She was turning into an old boring person or something, but she just couldn't shake the feeling that going to the club would have been more fun with Carter by her side.

Needless to say, she hadn't gone back to any clubs after that night.

"No," she told Debbie. "It's really not a big deal, guys."

"Is this about Carter?" Sharon asked, because Sharon was a traitor.

"Carter?" Melanie perked right up. She'd been half-asleep at Debbie's feet, having worked night shifts all week for some reason that Leticia had forgotten—because she'd been preoccupied thinking about Carter. "Who's this guy? Did Leticia finally find someone?"

"Sort of," Leticia replied.

Ross snorted. "Right, because having lunch together every day and a standing date on Friday and him bringing you coffee every morning is only 'sort of' dating."

"You told him?" Leticia asked, rounding on Sharon. "Your best friend status is revoked! Tom is my best friend now! And you—" She added, turning to Ross. "Like you have any room to talk, after all the stunts you pulled. How long were you two dating before you proposed?"

Ross put his hands up as if to say, "I surrender."

"Oh my God, are you dating someone?" Jonas demanded. "Are you dating somebody and you didn't tell us? This is betrayal."

"It gets even better," Sharon said with glee.

This was revenge for all of the times Leticia had made Sharon go to a college party or a club when she hadn't wanted to, she just knew it. That was the only explanation for this traitor behavior.

Everyone looked at Leticia expectantly, waiting for her to spill the beans.

With a final glare at Sharon, Leticia did. She reminded them how she and Carter met, and filled them in on how everything had gone since he'd gone from 'coworker I accidentally slept with' to 'coworker I'm accidentally dating'.

"This is hilarious," Debbie said.

"I think it's sweet," Tom replied, because Tom was the best human being in the whole wide world. "And rather mature, given how allergic Letty is to adult human emotions."

Never mind. Tom was also a traitor and could go sit in the corner and think about what he'd said.

"Sharon knows all about that," Leticia said, when she'd finished. "I told her last week. But the rest of what I'm about to tell you is all new, to her as well."

She then told them about the Friday date, and Sharon's advice, and calling Carter the next morning.

"Wait, you said his daughter answered the phone?" Ross blurted out. "He has a daughter?"

"Well fuck me," Debbie muttered.

"I suppose it's not as bad as being secretly married?" Melanie offered. "To a spouse that's alive, I mean."

"Thanks, I really needed that reminder," Jonas snapped at her.

Jonas had once dated a guy who had actually been married to a woman and in the closet about his sexuality. He had failed to tell Jonas this until six months into the relationship. Jonas, apparently, was still bitter about it, which—well, given her current situation, Leticia could hardly blame him for.

"Yes," Leticia said, confirming what Ross had asked and ignoring the peanut gallery.

She told them how the phone conversation with Molly had gone, and then she finished.

Everyone stared at her for a beat.

"And?" Sharon finally prompted.

"And what?" Leticia replied.

"Did you talk to him about it?" Melanie asked. "I mean, this was Saturday morning. As in last Saturday. You've had an entire week at work to talk to him about this. How did it go?"

"I didn't talk to him about it," Leticia replied.

Everyone groaned.

"What?" Leticia demanded. "He obviously didn't take me seriously enough to tell me about his daughter. I'm not going to waste time on someone like that. We can just be coworkers, it's no problem."

"Oh yeah, you seem totally unaffected by this," Debbie replied sarcastically.

Leticia huffed at her. "What do you want me to say? That I'm upset that he lied to me? I'm upset, okay? I trusted this guy. He seemed like a really decent person. Now it turns out he's got a daughter that he didn't tell me about—and that's pretty damn important. That's not really a small thing to hide from somebody.

"I mean, I knew he was private. I accepted that. But you'd think with all the time we've spent together over the last few weeks that he would have brought it up at some point. And I know I don't like kids, but he didn't know that, so why keep it a secret from me? Am I that awful of a person that he clearly didn't want his kid around me anyway? Or did he just not care enough about our relationship and where we were going to mention her? Because, you know, you don't talk to your kid about someone you're going to dump real soon. I was probably just a fun coworker that he also enjoyed sleeping with."

Leticia realized that she was starting to rant and cleared her throat, forcing herself to sound casual. "I mean, honestly, the lying gets to me but it's not a big deal. I can't even handle kids all that well, you know, so it's a good thing. I like him, sure, but there are plenty of other great guys out there that don't come with a bunch of issues—apparently—and don't have kids."

She shrugged, hoping that she'd managed to play it off as something she really didn't care all that much about.

Judging by how everyone was looking at her and the fact that Tom wrapped an arm around her shoulders, she had a feeling she hadn't succeeded.

"Oh, hon," Debbie said. "You sound like me when I was trying to convince myself I wasn't in love with Melanie."

"Aw, babe," Melanie said, smiling up at Debbie endearingly.

"I'm not in love with Carter," Leticia replied. "That's not what's happening here. It's way too early for that sort of crap."

"I'm sorry, who are you?" Sharon asked. "Is this the same person who told me to go after Ross and to stop being in denial and fight for my man and all of that? You're now calling that crap?"

"What, no, I'm—this isn't the same thing at all!"

"Sure it isn't," Jonas said, rolling his eyes. "You and Sharon, honestly. At least Debbie was honest about her pining."

"Well, I'm not pining," Leticia insisted. "There is no pining happening here. I'm just frustrated that apparently I'm not considered enough of a serious prospect for someone to consider introducing me to his kid."

"Letty," Sharon said gently, "It's okay if you have feelings for him. It really is."

"Does he know that you talked to his kid?" Melanie asked. "What was her name?"

"Molly," Leticia replied. "And I don't know. I'm not sure? Maybe? He seemed confused by my behavior this week."

"What was your behavior this week?" Ross asked.

"I just treated him like a coworker," Leticia replied. "That's all he wants and so that's all he's getting. I'm not going to waste my time on someone who considered me a convenient fling."

"Says the woman who was constantly having one-night stands," Jonas pointed out. "Now you're holding out for a man who will be serious and monogamous with you? Who are you and what did you do with Leticia?"

"Ha, ha."

"I can't believe you didn't talk to him about this," Melanie said. "How do you expect to get anywhere if you won't tell him how you're feeling and what you found out? The poor guy's floundering around in the dark."

"I didn't see the point," Leticia admitted, which was only half of the truth. The full truth was that she was scared. Scared to deal with this, to confront Carter, because if she did it would mean she'd have to admit how much this relationship meant to her—and she couldn't do that. If she did that, then she'd have to admit how much she was truly hurting.

She couldn't handle that.

"He's made it clear that this is just a fling, y'know?" She said. "And honestly, it was just having fun. What's the point in pursuing something that isn't going to go anywhere?"

"You don't know that it's not going to go anywhere," Melanie pointed out. "Not until you try."

Leticia didn't want to try. Or, rather, she didn't know if she wanted to try or not.

"Hey, who the hell finished off the mint chip ice cream?" Sharon demanded, striding into the kitchen.

Debbie immediately protested that nobody had said they wanted more of the ice cream, she had asked, and Sharon replied that Debbie obviously hadn't asked loudly enough—and Leticia took it for the planned distraction that it was.

Sharon was back on the best friend team.

With everyone sufficiently distracted over dessert, Leticia felt like she could breathe a little more easily. So what if Carter didn't take this whole thing seriously enough to introduce her to his daughter? That was his business. He certainly hadn't bothered to corner her on why she was behaving oddly that week.

Sure, she'd made it difficult for him, but all he had to do was back her up against the doorway or sit down at her desk and refuse to leave. If he'd really wanted to talk to her, he would have found a way, but he didn't. He just took her at her word and didn't even bother to find out what was wrong or fight for her.

If that didn't prove how invested he was—or wasn't—in the relationship, then what did?

Sharon sat down next to Leticia once everyone had moved on, chatting amicably amongst themselves while Ross set up the movie for the night.

"You okay?" Sharon asked, cuddling up to her.

Leticia laid her head on Sharon's shoulder and sighed. "I think so."

"We just worry about you," Sharon told her. "We can tell this is upsetting you. We want you to see if you can fix it. He obviously means a lot to you."

"He can't mean a lot to me," Leticia admitted. "Because that means I lost something important. I can't handle that."

Sharon sighed. "I know, sweetheart, I know."

She wrapped an arm around Leticia's shoulders, and that was where Leticia stayed for the rest of the night.

CHAPTER 14

Carter was admittedly distracted Saturday morning. It had just felt so weird to not have anything to do on Friday night. With all of Leticia's strange, distant behavior, he hadn't even dared to suggest a date that night. Why would he when she wouldn't even get lunch or coffee with him?

He considered sending her a text over the weekend, something that might break the ice.

Hal says that you get the coffee shop in the divorce, so feel free to start going there again.

Something like that, maybe?

But he didn't know how Leticia would take it. He was wondering if he ever really knew Leticia at all, if she could turn on a dime like this and he couldn't begin to figure out why.

"Are you okay?" Molly asked. She was sitting at the kitchen table, reading a book.

Christ, if Molly had noticed, that meant he must really be dwelling on it.

"Oh, nothing," he replied. "Just work stuff."

"Is there an important exhibition coming in?" Molly asked. "Are you going to have to start working on weekends?"

"What? No." Carter shook his head. "No, I don't think so."

The museum was open on Saturdays, although closed Sundays, but the rule was that the head and assistant curator got the weekend off and would only be called in if there was some kind of emergency. Otherwise, the head of security handled things.

"Okay. I thought maybe you had work 'cause your boss called last Saturday and now today's Saturday and you're all stressed." Molly went back to reading her book.

Carter nearly dropped the bacon pan. "Wait, what? Leticia called last week?"

"Yup!" Molly looked up again and smiled at him. "She sounded nice. She wanted to talk to you but you were in the shower so I told her she could wait. But she said it was okay and she had to go."

Something of his shock must have shown on his face, because Molly's face fell. "Was I supposed to tell you that? I thought she would call you later. I'm sorry."

"Oh, no, pumpkin." Carter shook his head and sent her a reassuring smile. "You did everything just right. Don't worry about it. I'm just surprised, that's all."

"Okay!" Molly beamed at him and then went back to her book.

Carter tried to focus back in on making breakfast. Leticia must have called him to ask about his behavior Friday night. He should have known that she wouldn't wait until Monday to talk about it— that was stupid of him to think otherwise. He should have given her some kind of explanation or something to keep her from worrying over the weekend.

But, hold on, why should he? Why was it so bad if Leticia called and Molly picked up the phone?

This all worked out for the best, didn't it?

Leticia was obviously pulling away because he had a child. It seemed that her mention of not being good with kids meant that she wasn't even really willing to try. Talking to Molly must have scared her off and... well... that was a good thing. He couldn't be with someone that wasn't one hundred percent invested in Molly as well as Carter. They were a package deal. If Leticia couldn't love his daughter as much as she loved Carter, then there was no point in continuing the relationship.

Not that—Leticia didn't love him. He didn't love her. This wasn't—they weren't even at that point yet. But it was always a possibility, wasn't it, when you entered a relationship? That was why you entered into a relationship, after all, to see if this was the person you would come to love.

Unlike other people, Carter couldn't afford to play around. If someone wasn't going to accept Molly, then he couldn't accept them. Plain and simple.

He'd just have to say something on Monday, something that officially ended things. He knew he wasn't the best when it came to talking about himself but he did believe in communication between people. And they were coworkers. He'd just...stop by her office, mention the coffee place again, because Hal was seriously upset and missing her, and then he'd say something about how she didn't have to explain, he knew why she was distant, and he thought it best that they just remain coworkers as well.

Perhaps, in time, they'd work their way up to friendly lunches again?

That would take time, though. It hurt him that Leticia had so easily written him off once she knew about Molly. That would take time to heal. But he could talk to her about it when Monday came.

Then Monday came, and he found that he couldn't do it.

He didn't stop by the coffee shop. He drove right to the museum and just hoped that Leticia had stopped by the coffee shop and said hello to Hal. If not, he'd have to give Hal her number so that Hal could text her.

When he got into the museum, Leticia was in her office. He could tell because the light was on. But her door was closed.

He raised his hand to knock, to start the day right... But then, he couldn't do it.

Why ruin the day if things went wrong? He could just as easily talk to her at the end of the day. That way, if it turned into an argument, at least it was at the end of the day and they could part ways immediately afterward and not have to deal with one another until they calmed down the next morning.

Carter left Leticia's office door untouched and went into his own office to start his workday.

He didn't see much of Leticia, although it didn't seem as though she was deliberately avoiding him. It occurred to him how many times throughout the day she had made a point to see him or he had made a point to see her. They would work in the same office or he'd tag along with her as she went through the museum. He'd pop into her office to pull her in for a quick kiss, and they'd get lunch every day.

Now that Leticia was keeping to herself and he wasn't making a point to see her, he hardly saw her at all. It was a lot more like how his previous job had been, working mostly by himself. At first he thought that he'd welcome the peace and quiet.

Then he realized how much he'd gotten used to seeing her.

He missed her, he realized, when the time came for lunch. Leticia somehow managed to get in and out of the museum without him noticing her, so he had no idea when she went to lunch or where. But he hated going out to get lunch on his own. He didn't go to their usual Thai place, or any of the other places they'd been together, just in case Leticia was there as well. He didn't want things to be awkward—or more awkward than they already were, anyway.

In the end, he got lunch in the museum cafeteria. It was incredibly boring.

When evening came and it was time to close up and head out, he started for Leticia's office again. He knew that she would still be in there. She always stayed later than he did. Partially this was because he had to leave by a certain time to pick Molly up unless he'd arranged for her to hang out at friends for a while after school. He'd been doing that more frequently as he ended up having dinner with Leticia, but no more of that.

Still, whenever he left alone, Leticia was still working. And it wasn't just because he had to leave for Molly. Leticia honestly stayed late because she cared about her job and she worked harder than anyone else in the museum and still managed to have fun.

Carter cut himself off from any more rambling. She was there, was the point. She was in her office. All that he had to do was knock and enter and talk to her and this would all be sorted and done with.

But he couldn't.

He just…something in him held back. Why did he even have to talk to her anyway? She'd made the decision to pull back. This was on her, not him.

And if he felt oddly bereft throughout the next few days, well… that was just how it was.

It took him until Thursday to realize that he was pining.

God dammit.

He didn't need to pine over someone who wasn't going to commit to his daughter. No way. There were plenty of other women that he could date, if he was so gung-ho on dating. Why would he have to commit to one woman completely, anyway? Why not go on a few casual dates, ease back into it, instead of immediately trying to find some replacement for Olivia? Not that anyone could ever replace Olivia. And, that wasn't what he was trying to do…

For fuck's sake. He was just kidding himself. Talking in circles to distract himself from the truth.

He missed Leticia.

She was unfailingly polite to him and cheerful in the mornings. He noticed that she was getting her coffee from Hal's coffee shop again, which was good. They must have figured that thing out on their own. But she would send him memos through email instead of in person. She wouldn't have lunch with him. She wouldn't stop by to say good-night, and her office door stayed closed rather than open, telling him in no uncertain terms that he wasn't allowed to approach and say goodnight or anything else either.

He hadn't realized how much Leticia had become a part of his life until she was gone. Now that she was, he found that his days were a lot emptier. There was less laughter in them. Definitely less sex, but that was only part of it. Leticia was such a driven, insightful person, the kind who was full of hard work and dedication to her job, but also full of fun and sass.

It wasn't as though his life had been empty before meeting Leticia. Or rather, it had been empty, but he hadn't known it. He hadn't been ready before, but now he was ready for someone like her. And to have her and then lose her...

His life had just been more full and more fun when she was in it. And now that she wasn't, it felt empty and dull.

But you know what? That was her choice. He had to just remember that. She had chosen to give up on him and on Molly and he couldn't change her mind about that. He wasn't going to give up or compromise on anything when it came to Molly, and if this was the way it had to be, well, then fine. He'd find the right partner, and the right mom, for Molly eventually. He just had to be patient. Trial and error—wasn't that what this was all about? That was what his life had been like before Olivia. Olivia had been far from his first girlfriend, after all. He'd gone through about five girlfriends before her. This was just the same thing.

And if he missed Leticia, well, he'd get over it. He was a grown man, for crying out loud.

Just give it some time, Carter thought to himself. You'll be just fine.

CHAPTER 15

$\mathcal{L}$eticia flipped through her file. All right, she could work with that. She'd have to move the Leiversham meeting to one o'clock tomorrow in order to oversee the delivery because God knew that, despite supposedly being professionals who did this every day, deliverymen never seemed able to do anything without damaging something unless she was around.

Of course, that might have something to do with how unique art pieces were. They could be hard to handle properly unless you knew what it was supposed to look like and the materials and how all the parts interlocked together.

All right. So. Move the meeting tomorrow to one. Watch over the delivery at noon, make sure it was installed…

Leticia froze as movement out in the hallway caught her eye. It was a child, a small girl.

Why was she back here in the office area?

Leticia looked around. There wasn't an adult in sight.

Getting to the offices was definitely not something that someone did by accident. You had to go up to the second floor, then go behind one of the doors clearly marked *Do Not Enter* or *Staff Only*, and then you had to get down at least one hallway before you got to Leticia's office, where this girl was.

Hmmm.

"Excuse me?" She called.

The little girl turned. Leticia couldn't be sure how old she was. Six? Seven?

She was a cute little thing, Leticia had to admit. Blonde hair, big blue eyes, and a tiny button nose. She looked like a regular advertisement for a department store or something. The quintessential American child.

"Are you lost?" Leticia asked, coming to stand in front of her.

Oh. It probably made the kid uncomfortable to be craning her neck up at Leticia like that. Leticia crouched down so that they were at eye level.

"Hi," the girl said. "I'm Molly. I'm looking for my dad?"

Oh, Christ. This was Carter's daughter. The reason that he didn't want to be with her anymore. The reason that he'd lied to her.

This should be fun.

"Well, hi, Molly," Leticia said. "How did you get all the way up here? Aren't you supposed to be in school?"

"Yeah, but we're on a field trip," Molly replied.

"Sounds to me like you should be on the tour," Leticia said, "And not going into areas where kids aren't allowed."

This was why kids drove her nuts—what was the problem with following rules? Okay, so Leticia didn't follow many rules herself, but still.

"But I've already seen everything," Molly said. "I knew everything the tour guide was gonna say. Daddy's taken me here so many times. I was bored."

Leticia couldn't really argue with that. "Okay, fair enough. You like art that much? Or just your dad?"

"No, I love art!" Molly replied. She set her backpack down and unzipped it, pulling out a notebook. "See?"

She handed the notebook to Leticia, who flipped through it. "This stuff is actually really good." She cleared her throat, knowing that her tone of surprise probably came off as condescending. "Sorry. I just—these are just really good, for a kid your age."

"My dad lets me practice a lot. He says I'm like Artemisia Gentileschi."

Leticia raised an eyebrow, impressed that Molly could both say the name and that she knew who the artist was. "You seem to know a lot."

"My dad works in art museums," Molly said, as if that explained it, and maybe it did. But just because Leticia's mom was a teacher didn't mean she knew tons about the education system. She was still allowed to be impressed.

"All right, Molly." Leticia stood up. "Put that away, and I'll take you to your dad."

Molly beamed at her. "Thanks!"

"But don't expect me to defend you if he's upset that you gave the school group the slip," Leticia warned. "They're probably all worried about you."

"Nah, they don't pay attention to me. Because I'm quiet." Molly shrugged.

"There's nothing wrong with being quiet," Leticia replied. "My best friend, Sharon, she's real quiet most of the time."

"Yeah, but everybody thinks it's 'cause my mom is dead. And I'm just quiet. It's who I am. But they think it's because I have no mom so they leave me alone and pretend I'm not there."

"Oh." Leticia didn't know what to say to that, especially when it was delivered in such a casual tone. "Well, I don't think that people should judge you for that. You know, growing up, a lot of people wouldn't talk to me because I was from Mexico."

Molly looked up at her with round eyes. "But that's not nice!"

"You give me hope for the next generation," Leticia told her. "Oh, look, here's your dad's office."

Just in time, too. Civil rights were not a topic she wanted to get into with a seven-year-old.

Leticia knocked on the door. Carter answered it, and for a moment he looked confused—which he had a right to be, seeing as she'd basically been avoiding him for the past couple of weeks. But then his gaze dropped down and he saw Molly.

If Leticia had any doubt that Carter cared about his daughter—and she hadn't had any doubts, but if she'd had them—they would have been washed away by the look of joy, then the look of horror, then the look of fond resignation on his face as he realized in rapid succession what Molly must have done.

"I forgot that they had a field trip here today," he said to Leticia before looking at Molly. "Molly? What is this?"

"I wanted to see you," Molly said. She stood firm and looked like she was daring him to get mad at her about it.

Leticia had to hold in a snort of amusement. She had to admire the girl's stubbornness.

Molly crossed over to Carter, hugging his leg as though that would make everything better. Judging by the delighted smile Carter gave as he looked down at her, looking as if he were smiling and happy in spite of himself, Leticia had a feeling that Molly's ploy was a success.

Carter looked up, shuffling his feet a little. Leticia hadn't ever seen him look so awkward. "Thanks for, uh, thank you for bringing her here."

"It wasn't any trouble," Leticia told him. "She was nearby. Apparently, she's quite the artist."

"I showed her my drawings!" Molly told him. She beamed, proud that she'd shared her work. Leticia wished that more artists felt like that. So many of them, even Tom, felt like they had something to prove. They felt that, if they shared their artwork ,it would be judged, so they had to be aggressive about it, perfect about it, screaming their vision from the rooftops instead of simply sharing it because they loved it and wanted to.

She hoped that Molly could hold onto that joy even as the rest of the world tried to get to her.

Leticia looked back at Carter. "Seriously, though, it was no problem. Don't worry about it. I'm just glad she's safe." There wasn't too much that Molly could get into at the museum that would lead to bodily harm, but there were plenty of alarms she could have accidentally tripped, never mind the fact that kidnapping was always a possibility.

"I really appreciate it," Carter repeated. Then he looked down at Molly. "All right, you, we have to get you back before your teacher realizes you're missing."

He glanced over at Leticia. "And what do we say to Leticia?"

Molly gave a happy little gasp. "You're Leticia! You're much prettier than I thought you'd be."

Leticia was startled into laughing. "What did you think I'd look like then?" She asked.

"I thought you'd look like my dad's old coworkers. None of them were young and pretty."

Carter rolled his eyes. "Molly, that's not at all nice to say."

"But it's true!" Molly replied.

"Even if it's true, we don't have to say it if it's not nice," Carter said. "Now, say thank you."

Molly smiled up at Leticia. "Thank you!"

Leticia tried to smile back. She probably looked incredibly awkward about it. "No problem."

She looked back at Carter. This was the longest conversation they'd had in the past couple of weeks. She suddenly found herself wanting to shuffle her feet the way that he had, feeling wrong-footed somehow. "I'll leave you to it then," she said. "And just…"

Leticia gave a wave—why did she wave? What was that? —and then backed into her office and shut the door.

Could she have been more awkward? She groaned and collapsed into her chair, putting her head in her hands.

This was her one chance with Carter, to show that she could be good with kids, and yet… she'd been a complete idiot.

Hold on. Who said that she wanted a chance with Carter? The guy hadn't told her about Molly. He'd obviously been awkward in front of her, uncomfortable with the idea of her being around his daughter. Why would she put herself through that? Why would she even want to be with a man who had a kid? She was always uncomfortable with kids. Case in point, her interaction with Molly. She was sure that Sharon or Melanie or even Debbie could have done much better.

Why, why did the guy that was so perfect have to come with something that made Leticia uncomfortable? Something that she'd never been good with?

At least it wasn't a baby or a toddler. A seven-year-old, sure, awkward, but she could handle Molly better than, say, a two-year-old. She could at least talk with Molly and interact with her without having to get into one of those illogical black and white arguments that toddlers always seemed to drag her into.

And since he already had a kid, that meant Carter probably wouldn't want her to have a kid. Which Leticia could get behind. She had never wanted to be pregnant, and she hadn't been a fan of the idea of adopting—not that adopting was a bad idea or anything. She totally supported adopting. She just didn't want to adopt a baby.

So, really, this was the next best thing to a guy who didn't want kids at all. But why would she deal with this when she could find said guy out there somewhere?

Leticia groaned. She was just chasing herself around in circles like a fox hunting an elusive rabbit. The truth was that she didn't want to go through the trouble to find some guy who may or may not exist when she had Carter in front of her. Carter was amazing. The sex was fantastic, she was comfortable with him, he was respectful and appreciative of her bold flirting and assertive nature, they worked well together at the museum, and she didn't get tired of spending time with him.

Somewhere, somehow, somebody upstairs was laughing at her.

It was probably her grandmother.

It didn't matter at this point, though, did it? There wasn't anything she could do to really prove to Carter she would be good with him and Molly, not when she wasn't even sure herself. Certainly not when it seemed that he had already made up his mind about her and them.

Still... that look on his face, the love that she'd seen washing over him when he caught sight of Molly. And then the horror that had followed right afterwards, the way that he had gone pale as he had realized what must have led to Leticia bringing Molly to his office door.

It was touching, honestly. She knew that parents loved their kids. She'd seen it before. Her parents, for one, would look at her and she knew that, even though she was an adult and had been for some time, they still saw her and would always see her as their darling girl.

Leticia felt herself softening towards Carter a little. Who wouldn't want only the best for their child? Leticia was far from a good role model. Carter had met her in a club, for crying out loud. She had said she didn't like kids. She was loud and brash and not exactly the best at balancing her schedule. She was a bit of a workaholic. Who in their right mind would look at her and think, 'Ah, yes, that's the kind of woman I want to be the stepmother for my child'?

Nobody, that's who.

Seeing his face when he caught sight of Molly, though... That moment of love... Part of her knew that she'd treasure that look for years to come. It was just so sweet. And when he'd looked down at Molly as she'd hugged his leg—like he knew that it was a shameless trick to get him to soften up, but he couldn't help but fall for it anyway because he loved his daughter that much—i

t gave Leticia a warm feeling in the center of her chest. She couldn't deny that.

Leticia straightened herself up. No use dwelling on it, she told herself. Carter had made his choice and she had made hers, and she couldn't entirely blame him for his. Molly was obviously important to Carter, beloved by him, as she should be, and Leticia couldn't get in the way of that.

She'd just have to make do.

CHAPTER 16

The next few days were quiet. Carter had stopped coming to the coffee shop and so Leticia felt all right going back there. She tried not to think about how the coffee didn't taste as good as it used to, because that would be ridiculous. Why would the coffee taste better just because Carter got it for her?

Hal could just quit it with the significant looks she was shooting at Leticia, as well. She didn't need Hal of all people judging her love life, or lack thereof.

"This isn't one of your fanfics," Leticia told her one morning.

"Never said it was," Hal replied brightly, ringing up Leticia's usual order.

Leticia looked at her suspiciously as Hal prepared her drink. "I'm not talking to you about it, either."

"I didn't ask you to," Hal replied, still cheerful.

Leticia narrowed her eyes. "But you want me to."

"Of course I'm curious," Hal said. "You two go from him buying you coffee every morning to you not showing up, and Carter obviously confused, and then no Carter and you here by yourself again. I can't help it if you two are the most entertaining thing about my day."

"You need more exciting days, then," Leticia replied, taking her coffee.

"Did you guys fight?" Hal asked, bracing her hands on the counter and leaning in. "Because I can help. I can totally be a go-between."

"What did I just say about me not talking to you about this?" Leticia told her. Ugh, why did this stupid coffee not taste as good? It was obviously psychological. She just had to remind herself that she'd liked this coffee just fine before she met Carter, and so she could like it just as fine after Carter.

So there.

"Oh, c'mon, you know I'm the best person to go to," Hal said. "I mean, who else knows both you and Carter and can be an unbiased assessor?"

"It's not like we had a fight," Leticia said, and then silently cursed herself for talking about it. She wasn't discussing it, dammit, not with her *much* younger barista who was probably roping the rest of the coffee shop crew into Harry Potter fanfiction.

Besides, how could she tell Hal that Carter had a kid? Was that really her business to say?

"Well, whatever it is, I hope that you two work it out," Hal said. "He's a really great guy and you're a really great girl. And he was concerned when you didn't come to the coffee shop. I mean, I was too, but. Yeah. He was concerned. I think he cares about you a lot."

Leticia didn't know what to say to that. If Carter cared so much about her, surely he wouldn't have just pulled away like he did on Friday, cutting off their relationship without a word, lying to her and hiding his kid from her?

But again, could she blame him? When having a kid was such a huge deal and she wasn't good with them?

"I'll keep that in mind," she told Hal, unwilling to break the girl's heart when she so obviously wanted them to make up.

Without Carter there to joke around with, Leticia's days were quiet. The way that they had been before she'd met Carter, actually. She hadn't minded the quiet before. Her work days had been busy, of course, but her work was mostly solitary except when she had meetings. She mostly dealt with things via email. It had been nice, a good juxtaposition between her work and her partying out at night. A lot of times she'd go to the club Thursday, Friday, and Saturday nights, even going out after she hung out with her friends unless they all stayed up too late. The craziness of the club had balanced out the quiet solitude of her work, and vice versa.

However, the silence and solitude that she had once found relaxing was now empty and hollow.

She hadn't realized how much Carter had come to fill every aspect of her day. He would stop by her office to deliver a joke or to do work with her, even though he technically didn't need to be by her side or could have shot her an email if he had a question. They got lunch together, of course, but there were all these little moments throughout the day when he would just stop by and make her laugh or drag her into a discussion or help her with an issue.

Now that camaraderie was gone. She'd been a part of a team, she realized. She'd had a genuine partner, in work and just in general, in life. And, now that she'd lost it, she realized how much she had needed it.

God, this serious relationship thing sucked.

She worked late, like always. Part of it now was because she hated the fact that she no longer had dinner with Carter to look forward to. It was like she had forgotten how to eat alone. She shot off a text to see if maybe Tom wanted a break from his artwork, or if Debbie had a lighter casefile load, but Tom had apparently turned his phone off again and Debbie was going to a movie with Melanie—which really meant she and Melanie were going to make out during the movie like teenagers and remember nothing of the plot.

Leticia didn't even try texting Sharon or Jonas. Sharon would be having dinner with Ross and Leticia just couldn't handle their couple-ness right now, and Jonas needed a full day's notice if you were going to take him out somewhere since he was a little OCD about making plans.

Instead, she decided to just work a little late that night and order takeout when she got home. There was always more work to do at the museum, so at least she wasn't hurting for things to fill her time.

She honestly hadn't realized that she wasn't the only one working late until there was a soft knock at her door. It was Carter—she knew that immediately. He was the only one at the museum capable of knocking 'softly' on anything. Mr. Horowitz tapped repeatedly and nervously, the head of security banged like zombies were on his tail, and the members of the board just barged in without knocking at all.

Leticia wondered why Carter would be working late. She felt a little bad about it, honestly. Now that she knew he had a kid, it was no wonder he always left earlier than she did and that he wasn't free on the weekends. He must have been sacrificing a lot of time with Molly in order to spend time with Leticia, and that hurt. She didn't want to be the reason that he wasn't giving Molly the attention she deserved.

"Come in," she called.

Carter opened the door and stepped in, closing it behind him. He looked a little tired, a little more worn than usual. Leticia hoped that she hadn't inadvertently been working him too hard. She didn't want to be that kind of boss.

"Everything okay?" She asked, genuinely concerned.

Carter sighed. "Can I sit down?"

Leticia nodded. Carter sat and stared down at his hands for a second. Leticia was wildly curious but kept quiet, trying to be patient. She half hoped that this was just something about work, but another part of her hoped that this would be about them.

"I wanted to apologize," Carter said. "I know that I acted strange on Friday, and that was probably why you called me and found out about Molly.

"At first, I was upset that you found out about her and your first instinct was to pull away, but I honestly can't blame you for making assumptions if I haven't told you the full story about things."

"I wasn't upset about Molly," Leticia said. She stood up and walked around the desk to perch on the edge of it, in front of Carter. She didn't want to do this with a big desk and computer between them. "I was upset that you had kept something so huge from me. It made me feel like…you didn't care enough about me to be honest with me. That you didn't trust me with this big part of your life."

"I understand, and I'm sorry," Carter replied. "I really get that. It wasn't that I didn't trust you, personally, I just… Molly was three when her mom died. It was really hard for her. She showed you her sketchbook, she said?"

Leticia nodded.

"I helped her start drawing as a way to cope with what happened. I told her that she might not have words for how she felt, but she could use art to express how she felt instead, and she didn't even have to explain her art if she didn't want to. Just that it was important for her to get those feelings out so they didn't build up inside of her.

"She didn't really talk for a long time. She's always been a quieter kid, you know, although she can get pretty bold around people that she trusts. She goes her own way. But she's not the popular kid, she doesn't speak up in class much. That's always been how she is. But after Olivia passed, she got even quieter for a while. She didn't want me to leave her side.

"About a year after Olivia died, I got the flu. I work in a children's museum, it's bound to happen sooner or later, right? Little walking germ factories, that's what kids are."

Leticia smiled a little in spite of herself. Seeing her amusement, Carter smiled back. Then he cleared his throat and kept talking.

"Anyway I get the flu, and Molly was frantic. I had my parents come over so they could take care of her and help her to keep from getting sick too, and I didn't even think about it until she broke down.

"She thought that I was getting sick the way Olivia did. My parents came over then too, to help out, and it all reminded her so much of her mom. She was convinced that I was going to die. It took forever for her to calm down and for me to convince her that I was going to be okay.

"She's really dealt with a lot, for her age. I mean, losing a family member is hard at any age, but I think it's a little harder when you're that young. You can't articulate what happened or how you're feeling and the world that was so safe to you for so long now seems cold, dangerous, and chaotic. All the things that your parents say to comfort you ring hollow. How could I possibly promise her anything when she'd already seen firsthand that nothing is permanent?

"In case you can't tell, I got pretty protective of her. And when I thought I should start dating again—my first thought was about Molly.

"Maybe if I didn't have her, I would have started dating again sooner. I love Olivia and I think a part of me always will but I got tired of mourning her. I know it isn't what she would have wanted for me. And when you're constantly missing someone, it just exhausts you. It keeps you in this kind of limbo. But so much of my focus was on Molly and taking care of her, and not just in a normal way, with how kids take up your life because they're kids, but with making sure she was okay.

"And so when I met you, I thought, well, I couldn't just start dating someone and introduce her to Molly right away. Maybe I should have told you about her, but I didn't know how to bring it up, and I was scared to introduce anyone to Molly right away because—what if we didn't work out? She'd lost a mom already and I didn't want her to start to believe that everyone in her life would leave her. Because you know how hard breakups can be. If Molly grew close to someone and then they broke up with me and then that meant they 'broke up' with Molly as well when she didn't do anything wrong..."

Leticia could see what he meant. That would be completely unfair to Molly, to get emotionally jerked around because of problems that weren't her fault and had nothing to do with her. There were a dozen reasons why someone would break up with somebody else and none of them would have anything to do with Molly—but she might see it that way.

Even if she didn't see it that way, it would be easy for her to believe that no woman in her life would ever stay. Leticia understood. Molly had already lost one mother. Why make her bond with and potentially lose another, and another, and however many until Carter found the right person? What if Carter never found the right person?

There were so many ways that it could mess Molly up. Leticia wasn't sure that she wouldn't have done something similar, if she were in Carter's shoes.

"I'm really sorry," she told him. "I just—I made an assumption. too. After I called you and Molly answered your phone and the way that you behaved on Friday night after I told you that you that I didn't get on well with kids... I assumed that you were pulling away because you thought I wouldn't want to meet her. That you'd decided that because I might not be good with kids, we were done. I was unfair to you and started pulling away too instead of talking with you about it.

"I'm not... I've never done a serious relationship before. As I told you. And I just—it was easier to pull away. To write you off. Instead of talking to you about it when I was...when I was really hurt." Leticia felt a bit ashamed of herself and swallowed down the lump in her throat. "I should have known that it would be a big deal for you to introduce Molly to a female friend or girlfriend. And I know that you had to go through a lot, grieving Olivia and helping Molly through her grief. I'm so sorry. I was really selfish and thinking about myself and making it all about me. That really wasn't fair to you."

Leticia felt her eyes go blurry. She was just so ashamed of herself. She'd been so selfish. Sharon and the others had been right; she should have talked to him about this. Really, a lot sooner. She wasn't stupid, she didn't think it would have meant they were still together. Molly was still a huge factor, after all. But it would have saved both of them a lot of trouble. It was still wrong of her.

"Whoa, whoa, hey," Carter said. He sprung up out of the chair and crossed the space between them, cupping her face in his hands. "None of that. I kept a big secret from you after we'd been dating for, what, a month? You had every right to be upset."

"I still should have talked to you."

"And I should have talked to you, so we're even."

She looked up at him, smiling in spite of herself. "You're far too sweet, you know that?"

Carter smiled back at her. "Yeah, well, that's why I picked a brassy girl like you. I can just sic you on people."

Leticia gave a watery laugh. She pulled him in, hugging him, holding him close. "I'm so sorry," she repeated. "About Olivia and all you had to go through. And for being selfish and not thinking about any of that."

Carter hugged her back tightly. "I don't want to hurt her," he admitted, softly, and Leticia knew he was talking about Molly. "I feel like it would almost be worse than losing Olivia. It hurt so much to know that there was nothing I could do to save her, but at least it wasn't because I made a mistake. If Molly ends up hurt or something, it'll be because I fucked up. I can't handle that."

"You're not going to," Leticia said firmly. She pulled back so that she could look him in the eye. "You're a great dad."

"You haven't even seen me with her, not really," Carter pointed out.

"I don't have to," Leticia replied. "I've seen how you are at work and with Hal and with me. You're a good person. I mean, you gave me the most thoughtful first date I've ever had. If you'll do that for a woman that you're just starting to get to know, then I know that your daughter has an amazing father. The look on your face when I brought her to you—God, I could see that she was your whole world. Don't put yourself down."

Carter gave a small, fond chuckle and shook his head. "How in the world do people manage to miss this side of you?" he asked wonderingly, and then he leaned in and kissed her.

It was an instinctive thing, Leticia knew. They'd been so close for a few weeks. Up until the whole thing with Molly had gone down, it would have been perfectly natural for him to kiss her fondly like this. Old habits die hard.

So she knew—she knew that she shouldn't be responding. She should pull back, should let him make his excuses and leave. The issue of Molly, of her not wanting to deal with kids, hadn't gone away.

But she was a weak, selfish woman, and she'd missed him. When he kissed her, she kissed back.

She opened her mouth to him, sliding her tongue across his bottom lip. Carter groaned, responding to her, his tongue sliding into her mouth possessively the way that made her shiver all over. His hands slid down to grab her thighs, wrapping her legs around him so he could grind against her.

"Yes," she gasped into his mouth. She'd gone over two weeks without sex now, without him, and her body was shifting into overdrive. "Please."

"Damn," Carter said, his hands roaming all over her, squeezing like he was trying to remember the shape of her. "God, I missed this."

"I haven't—" Leticia confessed, letting him suck at her neck. She thrust up against him, thrilling at the feel of him growing hard between her legs. "There hasn't been anyone, I want you so badly—"

"Yeah, yeah, hold on." Carter yanked her blouse open, exposing her breasts. He slid his hand in underneath her bra, lightly pinching her nipple. "I'll give you what you need, baby, promise."

"I'll be good," Leticia promised, already slipping back into old habits with him, ready to beg, wanting to hear him talk to her. "Please, Carter, talk to me, please—"

He kissed her again, deep and filthy, and she moaned into his mouth, rutting shamelessly against him and making his hips jerk erratically as she strained against the confines of his jeans.

"Look at you, being naughty," he whispered into her mouth. He let Leticia unbutton his shirt and tug it off of him so she could run her hands over his body. She'd missed this, missed feeling his muscles jumping underneath her touch and the tone of his skin and the way his muscles were hard and had no give when she squeezed them.

She had the sudden and swift image of them maybe doing a little student/teacher roleplay in the office and she let out a little gasp, clutching at Carter harder. God, he'd be so good at that.

"How do you want this?" Carter asked. He wouldn't stop touching her, his hands coming up underneath her skirt to tease along her stomach and thighs, refusing to get to where she needed him most. "Do you want me to bend you over? Or just like this?"

Leticia could easily picture Carter flipping her around, his hand sliding down to work her clit while he slid into her from behind. But she didn't want him to pull away. She was terrified that if he did, he'd remember all the reasons why this wasn't a good idea and he'd put a halt to it.

"Just like this," she told him. She kissed along the line of his shoulder, re-memorizing the taste of him on her tongue, the feel of him underneath her lips.

"Be a good girl, then," he said, "And touch yourself for me."

Leticia whined, but Carter took a hold of her legs and spread them wide. "Go on, show me how you do it," he told her.

He helped her shove some papers to the side—they were making a mess, but that was something for Tomorrow Leticia to deal with, not Now Leticia—so that she could lie back, avoiding the computer as he shoved her skirt up and pulled her underwear down. She loved it like this, her clothes still half on, Carter hurriedly undoing his pants, the dim lighting of the office. It sent a thrill through her, made her feel sexy, breaking the rules like this just a little.

She slid her hand down between her legs and began to touch herself. She teased herself a little, avoiding her clit, stroking her fingers through her folds instead and teasing a single finger in and out of herself. She was putting on a bit of a show for Carter, she knew, but it was so worth it for the way he was watching her, chest slowly flushing with arousal, his eyes dark and entranced.

Leticia bit her lip and laid back fully on the desk so that she could free her other hand up to work her breast through the lace of her thin bra, then trail her hand up and down her stomach and throat, alternating where she was touching but keeping it light and teasing.

"Look at you," Carter growled. He began slowly stroking himself, his gaze devouring her. "You're so gorgeous like this. I don't know whether to taste you or fuck you. I want to do everything to you at once."

Leticia squirmed a little, starting to touch her clit properly and sliding a finger inside of herself, getting herself ready for him. "I think about this all the time," she admitted. "I want—I want you to touch me, every way, all the time, I want to know what you want to do to me..."

"I don't think there's anything I don't want to do to you," Carter admitted. He strode closer and put his hands on her thighs, watching her as she slid a second finger into herself. "God, yes, keep working yourself like that. Being such a good girl for me, getting yourself all wet for me. Does it make you wet, when I talk to you like this?"

She nodded, a moan fighting its way out of her throat. "Yes."

"You want to hear about all I want to do to you?" Carter kissed along her stomach, right at the line of her skirt. "I want to put you over my knee and spank you until you're begging me to let you come. I want to tie you down and tease you until you don't even know your own name. I want to take you into the shower and kiss you like we're in the rain. I want to go so slowly that we're both dying for it."

Leticia rubbed her thumb mercilessly against her clit, whimpering. She wanted him inside of her so badly, she wanted all of the things he was telling her, and more.

Carter took her by the wrist and gently moved her hand away, moving to the side so that he had a good angle to slide his fingers inside of her. They were bigger, thicker than her own, and she keened. God, she'd missed this. Her own fingers were never enough to fill her.

"I'd fuck you underneath a hell of a lot of artwork if I didn't think we'd get in huge trouble," he admitted. He moved inside of her slowly, still teasing, his thumb only occasionally passing over her clit. Leticia clawed at him, moaning. That would be so hot, even if it could never happen because they'd get in so much trouble.

"C'mon," she begged. "It's been so long, fuck, Carter, please, I've missed you, please—"

"Fuck," Carter swore, bending over and kissing her. "I've got you, promise, I've got you, hold on."

He sped up, finally touching her clit properly, until she was gasping and clutching at him, white-hot pleasure blinding her inside and out. "Inside me, inside me, please, please, please," she begged. "I need it, I need you so badly."

Carter slid his fingers out of her and bent down to grab his pants, digging out his wallet and pulling out a condom. Leticia arched her eyebrows up and he coughed, flushing pink. "I just got into a habit of carrying them around, since we would...you know."

She thought it was adorable how he could go from talking dirty at her to blushing and stammering over a condom. And, it was true— they had gotten into a habit of quickies in the office. This was far from their first time doing it in the museum.

Leticia propped herself up and watched him. She tried to smirk, but she feared that it came off more as a fond smile.

She held out her hand as he approached, taking his hand and pulling him to her so that he could bend over her, between her spread legs. He positioned himself carefully.

"Let me know if I'm hurting you," he warned her, as if she wasn't already wound up after two weeks of nothing and having both her fingers and his fingers inside of her already.

"I didn't become made of glass in the last couple weeks," she huffed.

"Yes, but you also haven't had sex in the last couple weeks." Carter kissed her quickly on the lips. "I want to be careful."

"Get inside me," she begged. "Please. I'm okay, I promise."

Carter pushed her hair back out of her face and kissed her deeply. She moaned into his mouth and wound her arms around him as he finally, finally slid inside of her.

She'd missed this, fuck, she'd missed this so much. She missed him kissing her, and moving inside of her, and teasing her and talking to her.

Leticia wrapped her legs around him so that he could brace himself on the desk—thank God for sturdy ancient desks—and fuck into her deep and fast, the way that she liked it. She arched up to meet his thrusts, shifting one leg and hooking it over his shoulder, giving him more room so that he could bottom out inside of her.

"Yes!" She cried out. It was a good thing that nobody was around. The security guards focused on patrolling the art galleries, and rarely came up to the private offices. After all, what thief would want to go into the office? All the expensive art was in the galleries.

She kept babbling, crying out as Carter drove into her again and again, grunting and gasping her name. Everything was sharpened, heightened by the abstinence beforehand. She loved him like this, she loved him inside of her and touching her and driving her crazy and having this control over her. She wanted him like this all the time, she'd missed this, and missed him...

A part of her was lucid enough to worry about the things she was confessing. She was writhing in pleasure, lost, unsure of what she was just thinking in her head and what she was saying out loud. There were things that she probably shouldn't be admitting, given that they weren't together anymore but she couldn't—it was all too much and she couldn't—

She came, crying out, clutching at Carter and letting herself—just as an indulgence—scream his name.

Carter buried his face into her hair and groaned out her name as he came, which made her feel a bit better. If they were being sentimental saps when they had no right to be, at least they were doing it together.

They lay there for a moment, breathing quietly together. Leticia had missed this, too. She had loved just lying with Carter afterwards, coasting on the pleasure, easing their way down, joined together.

Panic hit her straight in the chest, curling up like a freezing-cold bundle in her sternum. She couldn't do this. She couldn't be that attached to someone who didn't want her, someone she couldn't be with because of her hang-up about children. She couldn't be a good mother to Molly, not to any child. And she couldn't possibly insist on staying with Carter when they both knew she couldn't give him what he and Molly needed.

She quickly turned her head to bury her face into the crook of Carter's neck. Just breathe, she thought to herself. Just breathe.

After a few moments Carter drew back and they grimaced down at the mess they had made, laughing at one another.

"God help the next person who has this office," Leticia said.

"We can never tell them," Carter said, sounding horrified.

They cleaned up and got dressed. A bit of awkwardness set in, as Leticia had feared it would.

"Have a good weekend then?" Carter said, as if it was a suggestion.

Leticia nodded. She'd forgotten that it was Friday. "Yeah, you too. Have fun with Molly."

It felt so weird to say, to mention Molly as if she'd known about her the entire time, as if this was normal.

They finished dressing and then hovered there, awkwardly. Leticia wondered if this was always how it would be between them now, if they'd be dancing around one another, more uncomfortable than when they'd first started working together after that one-night stand.

Carter strode forward after a moment and put his hands on her hips, kissing her gently. Leticia tried not to think about how it felt like goodbye—and not just a 'see you later' goodbye. A more permanent goodbye.

Leticia let him go. How could she do anything else? She didn't even know what else to do. What to say. How to act.

She waited until she knew he'd have gotten into his car and driven away.

Then she went out and danced until she could see the dawn.

CHAPTER 17

"Why are you here?" Leticia groaned. God, she hadn't been this exhausted and hungover in ages. She'd gotten very good at planning out her schedule when it came to clubbing. She hadn't stayed up until six a.m. in years, and she certainly hadn't had that much alcohol since two years ago when she'd puked her guts out over a bad bottle of tequila.

Bastards, not making tequila properly.

"I'm here because student loans don't pay themselves," Hal replied. She slid a cup of coffee onto the table. "Four espresso shots? Really? Are you trying to give yourself cardiac arrest?"

"Be grateful I'm not pouring an energy drink into this thing," Leticia said warningly. God, it felt like there was a throbbing egg inside of her brain that was going to explode any second.

"Let me get you something to eat. The cheese-and-egg bagel sandwich always helps me feel better." Hal walked over behind the counter.

"I am not eating your greasy, chemical-laden whatever," Leticia mumbled.

Hal returned a few minutes later. "I promise, it looks nauseating to you right now, but it'll help. Nice and warm and greasy and filling, 'kay?"

Leticia didn't quite agree with her, but it was better than keeping an empty stomach. Hal also helpfully plunked a bottle of water down in front of her, along with two Advil.

"You've dealt with this before," Leticia said wisely, quickly downing the pills and half the water bottle before moving onto the coffee and food.

"I'm a college student," Hal replied. "Duh."

Leticia didn't reply. Instead, she focused on getting everything into her stomach without it coming back up for an encore performance.

God, she'd been so stupid to go out that late and party that hard. If Sharon could see her, she'd be making a huge fuss, playing the mother hen. Which was why Leticia had bothered to drive to the coffee shop on a Saturday. She figured she could let Hal baby her a little, and be conveniently unavailable if Sharon or anyone else called and wanted to stop by her apartment or have her stop by theirs.

"So, what happened?" Hal asked.

"What do you mean?" Leticia asked. "I went out to a club—" Or five, but who was counting? "—and I had some fun. Danced. Drank."

"Did you pick anyone up?" Hal asked.

Leticia shook her head minutely, trying not to move her head too much. The throbbing had subsided. Now she just felt generally unsteady. "No."

She could have, she knew that. There were plenty of guys sneaking looks at her all night while she was out on the dance floor, letting the music move into her bones and vibrate in her chest until all other emotions faded away. But when she'd thought about it, all she could remember were the times that she'd gone home with someone only to have them treat her like a cheap hook up. She didn't want just casual sex anymore.

But she couldn't have what—or rather who—she really wanted, either.

Hence the dancing.

It had felt like, if she danced enough then, maybe, just maybe, she could forget the ache in her chest and the odd tightness in her face and the way she'd felt letting Carter walk out of her office door. The kiss that had tasted like goodbye.

Needless to say, it hadn't worked. Hence coffee and self-pity at nine o'clock in the morning on Saturday.

"Y'know, I've never seen you in here on the weekends," Hal pointed out. "And I know you're not a morning person but you're never like…" She waved her hand up and down. "This."

"What are you trying to say?" Leticia said, although she suspected that she knew what Hal was getting at.

Hal sat down, folding her arms on the table and balancing her chin on her forearms. "He really did a number on you, huh?"

"Just let me nurse my hangover in peace," Leticia replied, more sharply than she'd intended. She wasn't going to start moaning about her love life to someone who wasn't even out of college.

Hal just gave her a fond look, proving that she was a better person than Leticia deserved, and stood up. "Okay. But I'm always here if you want to talk."

She put her hand on Leticia's forearm for a moment, letting Leticia feel the weight and warmth of it, and then went on back behind the counter to do whatever it was Hal did when there weren't a lot of other customers. Inventory or something, probably.

The door to the coffee shop jingled and Leticia winced. The sound went straight to her headache like someone had fired an arrow directly between her eyebrows. She kept sipping her coffee and nibbling at the bagel sandwich as the new customer approached the counter.

"Oh, hey!" Hal said, and something about her tone made Leticia look up.

Standing at the counter were Carter and Molly.

Leticia felt like throwing up again—this time for an entirely different reason. Shit, just her luck that the guy she'd gone out partying to forget would decide today of all days to frequent the coffee shop again. Or maybe he always came on Saturday mornings and she just didn't know, since she never came here on Saturday before?

She didn't think Carter had seen her yet. His back was to her while he ordered at the counter. Maybe she could sneak out quickly before he turned around...

Molly was holding onto Carter's hand but gazing around the coffee shop with interest. She turned completely around, and then she saw Leticia.

Her eyes lit up.

Shit, Leticia thought.

Molly waved. "Hi, Leticia!"

If the earth had swallowed her up in that moment, Leticia would have said thank you and praised the Lord. As it was, the earth did not swallow her up, and she was a little more convinced that her grandmother had somehow taken over the afterlife and was orchestrating everything to punish Leticia for having her name but refusing to be like her (which meant getting married right away and having like five kids).

It was also entirely possible that she had unresolved family issues but she wasn't getting into that right now.

Molly kept waving until Leticia felt like she just had to wave back or it would get even worse, so she raised her hand and did a little wave. Hopefully now Molly and Carter would—but nope, it looked like Carter had ordered for here, not to go, so they were going to all have to sit in this coffee shop together and try not to stare at each other...

Or, Leticia thought, Molly could just take her dad's hand and march him over to sit at her table. That was apparently another possibility.

Seriously, had she accidentally run over a puppy or something and failed to notice? Where was this bad karma coming from?

"Hi!" Molly said cheerfully—and loudly. Leticia winced.

Oh, great, she was meeting Carter's daughter again and this time she had a hangover. She was just a shining example of womanhood, truly.

"Hey, kid," Leticia said, trying to smile. She was pretty sure it came out as a wince instead. "What brings you here?"

"Daddy forgot something at the museum last night so we came back to get it. He said to make it up to me I could get hot chocolate." Molly beamed and Leticia suspected that hot chocolate was a special treat.

"Sounds delicious," she said. "Did you get whipped cream?"

"Uh-huh." Molly nodded.

Carter sat down, looking as reluctant as Leticia felt. "Sorry," he told her. "We should not be intruding on Leticia's alone time," he added to Molly.

"It's fine," Leticia said. She didn't mind Molly too much. It was more that she was hungover and she was worried that Carter or Molly was going to notice.

"Thank you again for bringing me to my dad," Molly said.

"Yeah, no problem," Leticia replied. "Did you like the rest of the tour?"

Molly nodded. "I've seen all of it before, though. I like the Chinese art best. I've been trying to draw Chinese dragons, look!"

She pulled out her sketchbook, which seemed to be ever-present, and showed Leticia her drawings. "I can't draw any with five toes, though. Those were Imperial Dragons just for the Emperor."

"This is really good," Leticia said, examining the drawing. "Have you thought about being an artist when you grow up?"

Just talk about art, she thought. That was safe ground.

"Yeah, like my dad!" Molly said.

Leticia turned and stared at Carter. "What?"

Carter shook his head. "It's nothing, really—"

"No, he's really good, you should see his stuff!" Molly said. "It's abstract."

"I wouldn't even call it that," Carter said. He looked at Leticia. "It's not anything, honestly. It was just…a way to cope after Olivia. I never had any formal training or anything."

"I had no idea that you were an artist," Leticia said. Another secret that he'd been keeping from her.

"He won't show people," Molly said. "But you're the head curator, right? So you know art, right? So you can see it and tell him it's awesome because he won't listen to me even though I know art. I know what the golden mean is and disappearing horizons and spirals and everything."

"Teaching her about the Renaissance, I see," Leticia said to Carter, raising an eyebrow.

Carter coughed, his ears going pink. "I figured she might as well start if she was going to keep drawing all over everything and asking questions all the time."

Molly started going on about da Vinci and the rest and, for a moment, Leticia was bowled over. She had heard, of course, that children at a young age were basically sponges. They soaked up all information—it was why some parents pushed their children to learn higher math and sciences at a young age, and why young children were able to learn languages so easily. But she'd never really seen it first hand, especially not so articulately.

It was still a little awkward. She wasn't going to deny that. But it was great to find that she could actually talk to Molly, almost as if she were another adult. Leticia couldn't really discuss theory or debate DADAism with her or anything, but she could chat with her about the different periods of art history and share fun details about the lives of artists. Molly would answer with facts of her own and her opinions on various artwork. It was... easier than Leticia had expected, actually.

"We were going to go home and make macaroni and cheese," Molly said at last, when they'd finished their drinks. "Homemade. You should come home with us! Daddy can show you his paintings."

"I'm sure Leticia doesn't need to see those," Carter protested.

"Sure she does! And you'll love his macaroni and cheese, it's the best," Molly confided. "I hate the out of the box stuff 'cause Daddy's is so good."

"I fear I spoil her," Carter admitted.

"I don't want to impose," Leticia said. "I'm sure you and your dad have much better things to do—and I don't want to get in the way of your father-daughter time."

"We get that all the time," Molly protested.

Leticia waited for Carter to say something else, but to her surprise, Carter didn't protest. He seemed nervous about the painting aspect of it, but when it came to lunch he said...nothing.

"You won't be in the way," Molly said. "You like my art, if you want to see more of it, it's all over the walls."

Leticia looked over at Carter. Homemade macaroni and cheese did sound really good, actually, and might be better for her hangover than the bagel sandwich. No offense to Hal or anything. "Sure. If it's okay with your dad, that is."

To her surprise, Carter gave her a tentative, almost shy smile. "It's totally okay."

Leticia smiled back, feeling warmth spread through her chest. "Okay then."

Carter gave her directions to his place and they headed out. Leticia waved at Hal as she left, ignoring Hal's frantic facial expressions and attempts to mime words. She had a feeling that Hal was going to grill her about this come Monday morning.

As they got into their separate cars, Leticia tried to breathe properly. She could do this, right? Just spend an afternoon with Carter and Molly? While still a bit hungover?

...Yeah. This was going to be interesting.

CHAPTER 18

*C*arter was a bit uneasy about bringing Leticia home with them.

For one thing, bringing a woman back to his house was a big deal to him, even without factoring in Molly. Second, he was definitely nervous about showing Leticia his art. He'd never shown it to anyone before besides his Nan and Molly.

The art had been a way for him to cope with Olivia's death. He'd had a hard time expressing himself, since he'd been so determined to put on a brave face for Molly. He had allowed himself to sometimes show when he was sad so that Molly would know it was okay to grieve and to show emotion, but he'd never tried to show just how much he was hurting. He hadn't wanted her to have to deal with that. But talking to his friends and family about it had just felt exhausting. Why would he want to go over the same things with them when it felt like he was just talking in circles? How many times could he go to a friend and say, "I'm sad" or "I miss her"?

It had been Nan's suggestion to start painting. He'd told her dozens of times that he wasn't any good, but she had told him that didn't matter.

"Art is where you heart has always been," she'd told him. "So, let that be where you pour your heart into."

She had been right. While he still didn't think his paintings were anything worth selling, they had helped him to express his emotions and come to terms with his grief. Even after he'd moved on and his missing Olivia hadn't been as sharp, he'd continued to paint, finding it soothing and a way to handle any big emotions or frustrations he ran into in his daily life.

He'd shown them to Molly, of course. He didn't want to keep such a big thing from her, first of all. And how was he supposed to encourage her about her own art if he hid his away from her like a secret?

But the idea of showing his art to someone as knowledgeable as Leticia, someone who was a curator and highly intelligent and chose what art would go into the museum and be displayed, someone who had artist friends and went to art shows and galleries weekly—it made his heart race. He hadn't been this nervous about showing someone anything since his junior year finals, when he was pretty much convinced that he was going to fail AP Studio Art.

He was also nervous about Leticia and Molly spending so much time together when he knew that Leticia wasn't comfortable with kids. He could see that in how she behaved. Most people approached kids with an eager delight, a sense of joy that could easily be sensed. Leticia approached talking to Molly as if one word might get her sent to the guillotine.

As the conversation had gone on, however, and Molly had talked more about art, he had noticed Leticia opening up more. She had relaxed and chatted easily with Molly about art history.

It would be so easy to fall into the trap of the idea that Leticia could come to love Molly. He knew that he was biased because Molly was in a way his entire world and he loved her desperately, as only a parent can love, but he couldn't fool himself into thinking that one conversation equaled Leticia revising her stance on kids and coming to accept Molly as her own. And that was far too down the line to even consider. He and Leticia had been dating for, what, not even a month? It was silly to go down that road, even in his head.

Yet he couldn't avoid the truth: he missed Leticia. He wanted to spend more time with her. As if his giving in last night hadn't been enough of a clue. He shouldn't have slept with her, not when they weren't dating anymore and had barely talked at all about what the deal was with Molly—but he hadn't been able to resist her. He still desired her, all the time it felt like. Touching her again after going so long without her had left him feeling dizzy.

He wanted to date her again. He wanted to spend time in her office making her laugh. He wanted to get lunch together and buy her coffee in the mornings. The problem was that he wanted the Leticia part of his life and the Molly part of his life to meet in the middle and mesh, and he didn't know if that was possible, and now he couldn't stop himself from hoping a little.

Molly pulled Leticia into the house by the hand, pointing to all the art around the house. There were mostly prints of famous artwork. A few pieces were original works by artists that Carter had come across at art fairs and such, but he'd tried to fill his house with as much artwork as possible and prints were simply less expensive. Besides, it gave Molly the chance to be surrounded by famous works that she otherwise wouldn't get to see in person unless she traveled to Europe or something.

"And this is where my dad's art is!" Molly said, leading Leticia into the room that Carter designated as his art studio.

"Wow," Leticia said. The word was quiet, almost nothing more than an exhale. Carter shuffled his feet, feeling his face heat up.

Most of his work was abstract explorations of color. He had started with the idea of using color to explore emotion, and then moved onto the idea of color as representing an individual personality. A vibrant, orange-toned painting was named *Molly*, for instance, while a painting in various shades of gray was titled *Dad*.

Leticia was staring around her, mouth slightly open.

"They're not really much," he warned her. "You don't have to say anything."

Molly looked up at Leticia expectantly, a small smile on her face.

"Not say anything—?" Leticia shook her head. "Carter, these are amazing. I have some connections—not that you don't, but—you should totally put some stuff up in the local galleries."

"They're people," Molly said, pointing to the one named after her. "That's me. I told him, he should do an interview where he gets to know someone? And then do a painting of them. Like a portrait, but different."

Molly pointed at another painting, this one pink. "That's my mom."

If he was to paint Leticia, Carter thought, he would do her up in red. Vermillion. Something as bright and vibrant as she was.

"What's this?" Leticia asked.

She walked behind the door to where he had rested some abandoned pieces. That had been from when he'd made himself take an art class. Most of them were abandoned figure drawings, but one was almost finished. It had taken him months of working over and over again to get it to where he wanted it. His own technical skills had been lacking, of course, but it was also that there were times he just had to walk away. The emotions would be too much. He'd go back to painting his abstracts, and then when it wasn't killing him anymore, he'd come back and work on it some more.

It was a portrait of a woman. She had Molly's face, especially her nose, but her hair was a soft, downy brown and her eyes were hazel. He had drawn her sitting on the window seat, book in her lap, staring out the window.

Olivia had always loved to daydream.

"That's my mom, too," Molly said. "Isn't she pretty? I used to want to look like her but now I'm okay looking like my dad, too."

Leticia stared at the painting for a moment, then carefully set it down. "It's really something," she said.

"It's hardly Michelangelo," Carter replied.

"Nobody's Michelangelo," Leticia replied, almost offhand. "I can feel the love and sorrow in this painting. Really, Carter." She looked up at him, and to his surprise he saw tears standing in her eyes.

"You do a really good job of capturing what you're feeling on the canvas."

He rubbed the back of his neck, unsure what to say. "Thanks. I'm not really—I don't do figures and such, normally. But I wanted to do one, of her."

"I'm sure she loves it," Leticia replied.

Carter could feel his eyes starting to feel hot and knew that if they didn't change the subject soon the both of them would be crying and that would just set Molly off. "So, mac n' cheese?" He said, gesturing towards the kitchen.

"Yay!" Molly yelled, running into the kitchen to start grabbing ingredients.

Leticia grabbed his hand. "I really mean it, Carter. I mean, you don't have to sell anything that you don't want to. But if you do want to—this is really lovely stuff. People will like these. You should give it a go. I wouldn't put yourself down so much if I were you. It's really great work."

She spoke softly, but with such conviction—the kind of conviction that he had grown used to from her. Leticia's opinions weren't unchangeable, but they were strong. They also tended to be formed based on her knowledge. If she wasn't educated on something, she would freely admit to it. But Leticia was highly educated about art and firm in her opinions of what constituted high quality and crafts-manship.

Basically, if she was telling him that his art was good... maybe it was.

Not that he was going to rush out and hand it over to a gallery or anything, but... It was nice to think about. To consider that, maybe, he wasn't as bad as he'd been telling himself he was all of these years.

It was a nice thought.

He squeezed Leticia's hand, giving her a grateful smile. Leticia smiled back at him and, for a moment, the urge to kiss her was so strong, he could hardly stand it.

It all felt so natural: Molly in the kitchen banging around, Leticia holding his hand and smiling at him, standing in his art studio on a

Saturday. He could almost imagine that this was how his life usually went.

Then Molly yelled, "Daddy, c'mon!" And Leticia's face fell a little, and she let go of his hand, and he remembered the reality of the situation.

God dammit.

He went into the kitchen to help Molly start making the macaroni and cheese. "I got this recipe from my mom," he told Leticia. "I make it for Molly more than I probably should."

"I should've known you'd be a pushover," Leticia said, winking at him and sitting down at the kitchen table.

"What did you think of my dad's art?" Molly asked. "Did you like it?"

"I loved it," Leticia told her. "I love your art, too. You're very talented. I guess you get that from your dad, huh?"

Molly nodded seriously. Then she brightened up. "Oh! I haven't shown you my room yet!"

She grabbed Leticia's hand and all but dragged her out of the chair, pulling her up the stairs. Leticia laughed a little, and Carter noticed that she seemed a bit less stiff than before.

The two girls were upstairs for a minute or two, and then they came back down. Leticia definitely seemed more relaxed than before —not entirely in her element, but also not as awkward.

Molly definitely wasn't like most other kids, Carter thought. She was very articulate and talked more like an adult, thanks to all the reading she did on art. She was quiet and could be very serious at times. He wasn't sure how much of it was the loss of her mother and how much of it was just who Molly was innately, but maybe that extra bit of maturity was helping to bridge the gap between her and Leticia.

He certainly hoped so.

The two girls chatted while he focused on making the mac n' cheese, smiling to himself as Leticia gently pointed out holes in Molly's logic and helped her work through arguments about why she did or didn't like this or that artist.

"You're entitled to your opinion," Leticia said, "But you have to be able to say why you have that opinion."

Molly nodded solemnly and drank in everything Leticia said. It made warmth fill Carter's chest and the ends of his fingers and toes tingle with something a little like anticipation.

They talked about more lighthearted things as well—Leticia had an endless number of funny stories about artists. She censored a few of them, Carter noticed, having heard the adult-rated versions at previous lunches they'd had together.

As he served the mac n' cheese, he thought about how natural this was. How he wanted to have this every day.

The realization hit him like he was a puppet and someone had just cut his strings. His knees buckled a little and he had to sit down quickly. He hoped that neither girl had noticed.

He looked from Molly, who was giggling and listening with rapt attention, to Leticia, who was using her hands to gesture as she told another story.

They were interacting more naturally, perhaps more easily than either realized. It scared him a little, how easily Molly was taking to Leticia, but Leticia seemed to be warming to Molly as well.

Carter watched Leticia. Her noted her dark eyes and how they danced. Her thick hair pulled back into a braid. The way she used her hands to assist her words, her full voice.

He was in love with her.

He sat there, feeling limp, a broken puppet. He was in love with Leticia.

What the hell was he going to do?

CHAPTER 19

*J*onas used a tortilla chip to gesture, like it was a baton or something. "And that's it? You just, had a nice lunch? You can't give us more details?"

Leticia had come straight from lunch with Carter and Molly to Melanie and Debbie's apartment. They'd moved in only a month ago but unlike normal people who moved in by degrees, Melanie had made sure that the walls were painted, the lamps were installed, the furniture was bought, and every decoration was in place. It was definitely smaller than Sharon's place, but they all agreed that Sharon couldn't be expected to host everything all the time. Even if she was the best at it.

"What do you want me to say?" Leticia asked. They were all crowded around the kitchen table, eating the takeout that Debbie had ordered because she'd gotten buried in case files and forgotten she was supposed to cook.

"Um, how about something more about the kid?" Ross suggested.

"Molly," Leticia reminded him.

"Right, Molly." Ross absentmindedly passed Sharon the guacamole, doing that weird couple thing where he knew that she needed a refill without even looking at her. "I thought you weren't good with kids."

"I'm not, but she's not too bad," Leticia acknowledged. "But this isn't... I don't want you guys thinking that some switch was flipped, and I was suddenly really good with her or anything, or that all of a sudden, I was like 'Hey, I want to be a mom after all!' I just—she was okay. We got along okay. I didn't say anything inappropriate, I didn't make her cry, and I didn't get pissed at her. That's a success in my book."

"Does this mean that you two are dating again?" Melanie asked.

"I don't know," Leticia admitted. "I mean, we had sex in my office yesterday evening—"

"You what?" Sharon shrieked. "And you didn't think this was relevant information to share before telling us this whole lunch story?"

"Was that why you went out last night?" Tom asked. "I did wonder."

"Why would you wonder?" Leticia replied. "I always go out."

Everyone around the table shook their heads. "Not since you started this whole thing with Carter, you haven't," Sharon pointed out.

"And maybe I missed it," Leticia said. "Maybe I just wanted to go out. I can want a serious relationship and also want to go out dancing at a club. The two aren't mutually exclusive."

"No, they're not," Debbie agreed, "But when you stop doing one thing while you're with someone and then start it up again the moment that things go sour, that's usually a sign."

Leticia rolled her yes. "Look, all right, so maybe I was..." She struggled for words. "Maybe I was pining. Just the tiniest bit. But honestly—can you blame me?"

"And you really don't think that you two have a chance?" Melanie asked. "I mean, the guy still seems interested in you, from what you're telling me."

"I can't be with him," Leticia protested. "Not when I'm not what he needs."

"You are totally what he needs," Sharon replied. "Stop putting yourself down."

"He needs someone who will be a good mom to his daughter, and we all know that I can't be that."

"You don't know for certain until you give it a go."

"Who says I even want to be the mom to his daughter?"

"Fair question. Do you?"

Everyone else at the table was silent, their eyes going back and forth like a tennis match as Leticia and Sharon took over the conversation, their comments flung rapid fire at one another.

"I don't know."

"Well are you willing to try it out and see?"

"But what if it doesn't work out?"

"Then you at least know that you gave it your best shot."

"I don't want to ruin anything! I mean this kid's already lost her mom, I'm not going to be the bitch who waltzes out of her life and gives her more abandonment issues. Christ."

"And I'm just saying that I think you're better with kids, or at least with this kid, then you think you are. Besides, honestly, we're all just winging it, aren't we? I mean, God knows I have no clue what I'm doing and I'm about to have a kid, too. God help the poor thing with me as its mom. Are your intentions good and do you want to? That's the question. Because who can say if you'll do a good job or not? Not even Carter can say if he's doing a good job or not. So do you want to."

"I don't know."

"This is better than television," Jonas whispered to Tom.

Leticia sent him the middle finger.

"Well, why do you think you might? What's stopping you from saying no and walking away?"

"I don't know!"

"Oh c'mon, Letty," Sharon said, rolling her eyes. You're better than this. C'mon. What is stopping you from walking away. What's keeping you coming back, why did you go out to the club to work off steam."

"I don't know."

"I think you're—"

"You know your rapid-fire thing that you do with people to get them to donate money isn't going to work on me, right chica? I know you—"

"—and you need to just admit—"

"—because I do not need you psychoanalyzing me after you took one psychology class for your Gen Ed requirement sophomore year—"

"—why is it so hard for you to—"

"Order in the court!" Debbie demanded.

"All right, fine!" Leticia yelled. "I love him, okay!?"

Everyone fell silent.

Leticia quickly stared down at her plate, trying to control her breathing.

"I'm sorry," Sharon said quietly. "I shouldn't have pushed."

"No, it's fine," Leticia mumbled. "I needed to say it out loud."

Tom reached over and squeezed her hand.

"I love him," Leticia said slowly. "I just still don't know—with Molly—I don't know if I can be what she needs, or if I even want to try. And until I know that... I can't yank Carter around. That would be unfair to him and I won't do that."

"So what's your course of action?" Melanie asked.

"I don't know," Leticia admitted. "We can't date, that's for certain. I'm not—I won't—" She took a deep breath. "I mean, obviously we need to talk."

Debbie snorted. "Yeah, you think?"

Melanie lightly elbowed her.

"And I need to tell him—crap, I need to tell him that I'm not sure and that I don't think I can be what he needs. He needs a mom for his kid and I can't be that. So we'll have to just be coworkers."

"But you love him," Sharon said, her voice small.

Leticia quickly wiped at her eyes. "Not everyone gets their fairy tale ending, Shar. Just because you lucked out doesn't mean that everyone else does."

"If you're supposed to be together, then it'll work out and it'll become clear that's what you're meant for," Tom said. "If you're not meant to be, then you're not meant to be, and that's okay, too. You'll find the person you're supposed to spend your life with, and you'll know because the pieces will fall into place for it to happen."

"I agree." Melanie nodded. "You're supposed to fight for what you love but it shouldn't be something that tears you up with indecision. You have to be 'hell yes' about it."

Leticia laughed a little in spite of herself. "I'm sorry. I'm being a total downer here. You're all saints for putting up with me."

"You're our friend," Jonas said. "It's what we're here for, at the end of the day. To support you and remind you that it's going to work out. After all, you would and have done the same for us!"

"And this from the pessimist," Leticia said. She gestured at Jonas, who gave a half-bow.

"We'll be there for you, however the chips fall," Sharon said. "Just keep us updated, okay? When you talk to him, and I agree that you do need to talk to him, let us know how it goes, all right? Keep us in the loop."

"Yeah, you kind of sucked at that through this whole thing," Debbie pointed out.

"All right, all right." Leticia quickly blew her nose on her napkin. "Now let's talk about something less depressing, ugh."

Come Monday, she would talk to Carter. She'd look in the eyes of the man she loved, and tell him they couldn't be together.

God, Monday was going to suck.

CHAPTER 20

*M*onday morning started out normally. Or rather, it started in that nebulous new normal that had begun when she and Carter had stopped dating. Leticia got her coffee from Hal and dodged the questions that Hal tried to ask her about what had happened on Saturday and were she and Carter back together and how long had she known that Carter had a kid?

She got to the museum and said hello to everyone, and then dove into the paperwork on her desk. She heard Carter come in but she didn't stop her work. She'd talk to him about their relationship at lunchtime. Leticia had it all planned out in her head. She'd knock on his office door around noon. Ask if he was hungry. Offer to get lunch together down in the cafeteria. That way it would be easy for one of them to flee if things got heated or emotional or whatnot.

They would sit down, and she would say something like, "I hate to sound cliché, but I think that we need to talk about the two of us."

Leticia had rehearsed her lines in the mirror and everything. It had occupied most of her thoughts on Sunday, although she wouldn't admit that to anyone if they asked. Except Sharon. She could admit that to Sharon.

She had an entire speech worked out about how important Molly was to Carter, and how talented she was, and what a great kid she was. She was going to talk about how she had nothing against Molly personally, and how she'd enjoyed her time getting to know her on Saturday. Then she'd talk about how she just didn't think that she could be what Molly needed, which was a mother, or what Carter needed, which was a co-parent. She'd make it all about her—this was her problem, it wasn't anything that Carter or Molly had done—and she was really hoping that they could still be coworkers who worked well together, and maybe they could even work their way up to being friends.

The idea of being just friends with Carter gutted her. She'd have to see him all the time and not touch him. She'd have to chat with him without kissing him. She would have to take all of the things she wanted to say and do and shove those urges down deep where they couldn't mess things up any further.

Oh, God, and then there was when he started dating—because he would date, eventually. He was gorgeous and sweet. What woman wasn't going to date him? Most women loved kids. Leticia was sure that any number of women would be jumping at the chance to date a handsome single father who came with such a mature and sweet daughter.

And Leticia would have to watch from the sidelines. She might even have to offer advice or listen to Carter talk about his girlfriend at lunch or something. The idea made her want to stab someone, preferably this imaginary future girlfriend, right in the eyes.

But, no. No, this was the fate that she had chosen, and it was the right one. So what if the universe was playing a cruel trick on her? So what if she was convinced that she was in love with Carter and that, if not for Molly, she'd probably be saying as much to him right this second? Obviously she was wrong. She was mistaken in her feelings. Who knew? She might even get over him more quickly than she imagined. She could pick up a few guys at the club this weekend. Maybe sign up for a dating app or something like that. She would be fine.

Ugh, that all sounded flimsy even to her own ears. She was going to probably do something stupid and embarrassing like burst into tears in front of Carter and then it would be this dramatic scene and everyone would be staring and he'd hate her for doing this in public and—

The door to her office banged open. Leticia jumped, startled.

Carter was in the doorway and he looked a little wild. No, not wild. He looked terrified.

"Everything okay?" She asked, standing up. His eyes were wide and he was paler than she'd ever seen him.

"I have to go," he blurted out. "I'm sorry, I—shit, I gotta go." He ran a hand through his hair. He looked like he wasn't even seeing what was in front of him.

"What's going on?" Leticia quickly walked around the desk to approach him. "Christ, you look like you're going to faint. What's wrong?"

"Molly's school just called," he croaked. "She's missing. She didn't turn up for classes. She's nowhere on campus, they've looked everywhere—"

The bottom dropped out of Leticia's stomach. Oh God. Molly, a small, helpless young girl. Shit, she could be—anyone could have—it would be so easy to—

"Go," she said, shoving at him. "Go, find her, and tell me when you've found her and she's okay."

"I'm so sorry," Carter said. "I just, I gotta find her…"

"Do you need my help?" Leticia could feel panic welling up in her throat. "Two people is better than one, I can go to—I don't know, is there a park or something she likes that she might have gone to?"

"No, no you stay here, you're needed here," Carter insisted. "You're the curator, you can't just walk out. That could jeopardize your job."

"I think the board will understand if they know I walked out to help find a missing child."

Carter shook his head. "I don't want you to risk your job. I'll find her."

"Are you sure?" Leticia took his hands and forced him to still. "You look insane, are you sure you don't need someone with you?"

"I'll be okay, I promise. I just—I have to get out there. I have to figure out where she could be."

"Okay. Keep me posted though, please, let me know the minute you've got her."

Carter nodded, looking like his mind was already a million miles away. Leticia couldn't help herself. She grabbed him and pulled him in, hugging him tightly. "She's going to be okay," she promised. "We'll find her and she'll be okay. It'll all be all right."

Carter wrapped his arms around her, burying his face in her shoulder. His chest shook once, violently, and she felt his mouth open against her skin, the same way it did when he tried to stifle a moan as they had sex—but now he was stifling a much different sound.

Then he was pulling away, dry-eyed, nodding at her before he ran down the hallway and was gone.

Leticia's legs gave out and she sank against the wall. Fuck. Molly missing. A seven-year-old girl.

She remembered how Molly looked just this Saturday, just two days ago, smiling with a mouthful of homemade macaroni and cheese. Leticia's heart felt like someone had put it in a vice and was clamping down with all of their might.

Anything could have happened to a small, sweet young girl like that. Leticia's mind raced with horrible possibilities and she tried hard to tamp them down. It wouldn't help Carter or Molly to stand here and panic. She had work to get done.

Leticia marched over to her desk and looked at her stack of paperwork. She could handle this, no problem. This wasn't even a whole lot of work.

An hour passed and she had to give up.

She was getting nothing done. She was compulsively checking her phone every five minutes, just in case she'd missed a text from Carter. She was scrolling through news apps on her phone, working herself up even more as she waited to see if there was some horrible breaking story that she needed to know about.

God, what was wrong with her? It wasn't like she was Molly's mom or anything—

Huh.

Leticia sat back, thinking. Here she was, panicking over Molly, and honestly, genuinely, wanting nothing more than to see her again. She wanted to scoop Molly up into her arms and demand that Molly never, ever leave her sight again.

Was this what parents felt? Did this mean that she could be a parent too, maybe, with practice?

Ugh, what kind of selfish person was she? Molly was missing. She could be hurt or in danger. And here Leticia was, contemplating how this might be spun to her own benefit, how this might mean she could have her cake and eat it too. What kind of—

Her phone rang and she honest-to-God screamed.

Composing herself, and grateful that no one had heard that, she grabbed the phone. "Curator's office, how can I help you?"

"Hey, Leticia?" It was one of the guards at the front desk. "I got a visitor here for you. Little girl, goes by Molly? Says she needs to have an appointment with you."

"Molly?" Leticia's eyes got wet and her throat felt closed up. "Small, Blonde, with a blue backpack?"

"Yup, that's the one. She says her dad works here."

"Oh my God." Leticia stood up. "I'm coming, I'm on my way right now, don't let her out of your sight!"

She hung up the phone and promptly burst into tears.

Molly was all right. Molly was all right! She was okay and she was at the museum and—

What the hell was she doing at the museum?

Leticia ran down to the museum lobby, almost shoving past a couple of people buying tickets. "Molly!"

Molly was sitting on a bench, her legs swinging, looking around at the artwork. She smiled wide as Leticia approached. "Hi, Leticia!"

"Oh my God." Leticia grabbed her and pulled her into a hug, not even caring if it was too tight. "Oh, thank God, Molly, you had us worried sick, oh my God."

"You were worried?" Molly seemed bewildered.

Leticia pulled back. "Your school called, where the hell have you been?"

Molly stared. "Have you been crying?"

"Molly." Leticia put on her best stern voice. "How did you get here? Where have you been?"

"I used my allowance to take the bus," Molly said. "I wanted to talk to you."

"Your teachers are frantic!" Leticia said. "Your dad is out there looking for you!"

"But I need to talk to you!" Molly was starting to get upset. She pulled away a little so that she could fold her arms and glare. "I need to talk to you about my dad!"

Leticia buried her face in her hands. "Molly, really?"

"Yes, really!" And there was that childish stubbornness that drove Leticia up the wall. "Daddy doesn't talk about it but he needs somebody. I think he needs somebody like you. He likes you a lot—and I like you a lot, too. You make him happy. He talks about you all the time and I don't think he knows how much he talks about you, and I really like you, and I think that you need to come and live with us so that my dad won't be lonely anymore."

Leticia slowly raised her face from her hands and stared at Molly. It felt like she'd somehow woken up in an alternate universe this morning and had just failed to notice until now. "What? You want me to live with you?"

Molly nodded fiercely. "Yes. You can even share my bedroom."

Leticia couldn't help it. She felt so relieved, and frustrated, and touched, and Molly had offered to share her room and it was so adorable she could hardly stand it—she burst out laughing and hugged Molly to her again. This time, she felt Molly hug her back.

"Is that a yes?" Molly asked, looking hopeful.

"That's a, 'we're calling your dad and telling him you're okay,'" Leticia informed her. She stood up and offered Molly her hand. "C'mon, kid. Let's make sure your dad's hair isn't entirely gray by the time the day's over, hmm?"

Molly giggled. "Okay."

CHAPTER 21

*W*hen Leticia called him, Carter was completely lost. Molly's teachers had no idea where she'd gone or where she could be. He'd checked her favorite park, the library, the cemetery in case maybe she'd gone to visit Olivia, his parents' house, her friends' houses—nothing.

He'd answered the phone, thinking she was just asking him how things were going. "I still don't know where she is." He knew that his voice was breaking but he didn't care. His little girl, his precious, precious girl, she was gone and she could be hurt and this was every parent's worst nightmare and God it felt like he couldn't breathe there wasn't any air and—

"I've got her," Leticia said. Her voice sounded both giddy and like a sob. "Carter, come to the museum, she's safe and I've got her."

"Oh, thank you." Carter sank against the side of his car. Tears started leaking down his face and he quickly rubbed them away. He couldn't drive if he was crying. "I'm on my way."

"Okay, drive safely."

Leticia hung up, and he was grateful—he wanted to talk to Molly, but he also needed to drive and if he heard her voice he knew he'd just start crying and wouldn't be able to get anywhere. Oh God, the last hour had been the worst of his life. He felt a little bad, saying that, having lost Olivia, but he knew without a doubt that she'd understand. Molly was everything to Olivia and everything to him. He couldn't even begin to imagine what could have happened if he'd lost her.

He drove as fast as he could, silently daring any cop in the area to try and pull him over, and sprinted into the museum.

Carter found them in Leticia's office. He paused there for a moment, since it didn't seem like they'd seen him.

Leticia was more relaxed than she'd been on Saturday. In fact, she was like the Leticia that he knew, completely at ease and in her element. She was laughing at something Molly had said, and she was sitting on the floor, Molly's sketchbook in her hands.

Molly.

She was sitting in front of Leticia, beaming up at her, looking absolutely delighted. She was whole, and happy, and safe. She didn't seem to have a scratch on her.

"Molly," Carter croaked.

She looked up at him and smiled. "Hi, Daddy!" She jumped up, and then she paused. She looked at Leticia, and then back at him. "Letty says that I made you scared."

"You did." He nodded. "You really, really did. You can't go somewhere without telling anybody. What if something had happened to you on the bus, huh?"

Then the other part of what she said hit him. "Letty?"

"It's her nickname!" Molly said. "Her friends call her that, and we're friends, so I can call her that. She said."

She leaned in a little, conspiratorially. "She gives good hugs," Molly whispered. "You should get one from her."

Carter got down on his knees and opened his arms. "I'd like one from you first, if that's okay, Artemisia."

Molly giggled and ran into his arms. He hugged her tightly, as tightly as he dared, and if he let a few tears fall, well, he doubted that Molly noticed and he knew Leticia wouldn't hold it against him.

"I'm sorry I scared you," Molly whispered. "I just wanted to talk to Letty."

"Yeah? About what?" Carter pulled back but still didn't let go completely. He just might have to hold Molly all day. Just in case.

"Her moving in with us!" Molly said.

Carter looked at Leticia, alarmed, but Leticia just laughed. "She said I could share her room," she said.

He looked back and forth between the two girls—getting along, acting like good friends.

Maybe...maybe this could work out after all.

But he'd think about that later, after he hugged Molly some more.

CHAPTER 22

*L*eticia felt incredibly nervous as she stood at the door to Carter's house. She had felt kind of like she and Carter were in a good place after yesterday, but of course his priority had been Molly and she'd understood. She wasn't about to intrude on that. So she had just let things slide, even though she knew that they had stuff still to talk about.

Now it was the next evening and she was armed with takeout, dammit, and they were going to talk. They were going to sort out this entire mess once and for all and nobody was going to stop her. Including precocious seven-year-olds that were rapidly growing on her.

She hoped that Molly liked the calligraphy set that she'd bought her. It was to help her learn Chinese calligraphy painting, since Molly had said how much she liked it. It was probably a little old for a seven-year-old but, with Molly's talent, Leticia felt she could give it a whirl.

Well, there was no use in standing out here panicking. It was time to do this.

Leticia knocked on the door.

It was opened almost immediately, and she had to look down

when she realized that it wasn't Carter who'd opened the door, but Molly.

"Hey!" She took out the calligraphy set and handed it to her. "Surprise!"

"Cool!" Molly yelled. "Hey Daddy, Leticia is here!"

"I brought food!" Leticia called.

"Oh goodie." Molly was already staring at the calligraphy set like she wanted to take everything out and start on it right then.

Carter came to the door, and for the first time in weeks, Leticia saw his gaze slide appreciatively over her body. God, how she'd missed that.

"Special delivery?" She said, holding up the takeout.

Carter laughed. "Come on in."

The nerves in Leticia's stomach didn't quite dissipate, but they settled a little. She handed Carter the food—she'd gotten Indian, which Molly had told her was her favorite—and explained to Molly how the kit worked while Carter got out napkins and such.

"How was your day?" Leticia asked. Carter had taken the day off to spend with Molly. After yesterday, Leticia really couldn't blame him. She'd been frantic herself, she could hardly imagine what he had been going through. She never wanted to see that look of panic and fear on Carter's face again.

"It was fun!" Molly said. "We went to the park and saw a movie."

"And Molly knows she's going to have to do a little extra to make up for missing school, and an extra chore or two to make up for disappearing and having a lot of people worried about her." Carter added, looking at his daughter. He turned to Leticia. "How were things without me? Did you all survive?"

Leticia put a hand to her head dramatically. "Oh, we barely made it without you. I thought the place was going to crumble in your absence."

Carter rolled his eyes fondly. "Good to know I'm indispensable."

"Oh, definitely," Leticia said teasingly. Of course, she was talking about the museum… But she couldn't help but think that it was true. He was indispensable to her.

She could only hope that he felt the same way, that her growing ease with Molly was enough for him to want to take a chance on her, and on them, again.

Molly was saying something, and Leticia focused back on her. She also hoped that Carter would want to continue this so that she could spend more time with Molly. She was realizing that she honestly liked the girl. She definitely felt protective towards her, as yesterday had proven. Leticia wanted a chance to get to know her more, and maybe earn a bigger place in Molly's life.

And really, the kid had offered to have Molly share her bedroom with her. If that didn't deserve some good bonding time, Leticia didn't know what did.

She hardly knew where she'd even begin with telling her family and friends—the friends outside of her innermost circle, anyway. *Hey, remember how I said I didn't like kids? Well now I'm dating a guy with one.* But that was all speculation, and none of it would matter if Carter decided that he didn't want to give this another go.

The idea made Leticia want to cry. She wanted to be with him so badly, it felt like she was sick whenever she imagined him dating someone else, or being coworkers only, or having to try and be friends without anything more when all she wanted to do was kiss him and be held by him and touch him whenever and wherever she pleased.

She was getting ahead of herself, she thought. First, dinner. She could do that. Then, talking. They really did need to get better about talking about the big, important things, instead of just dancing around them or acting based on assumptions. They'd both been guilty of that.

Dinner was really nice, actually. Molly told Leticia all about the movie, some new animated film that Leticia had sort of noticed was playing but hadn't paid much attention to when a commercial came on. Molly had loved it, apparently, and quoted various lines, doing her best to imitate the voices of the characters. It was pretty adorable, actually.

Carter explained how they talked about communication and that if Molly wanted to talk to someone, she could call them or something to set up a time to meet, so that there would always be at least one person who knew where she was.

"If you had called Leticia and asked to come over and speak to her, she would have said yes," Carter said, looking over at Leticia.

She honestly wasn't sure if she would have said yes. She would in the future, of course, no problem but, up until yesterday morning, she had still been nervous and unsure around Molly, so she honestly didn't know what she would have said. But she knew the point that Carter was trying to make to Molly, so she nodded her head and said, "Definitely."

Anyway, it was true now. If Molly called and asked to see her, Leticia would only ask when and where.

The only bad part about dinner was Carter.

He kept touching her, and looking at her, smoldering glances that just barely skated the line of appropriate. Leticia didn't think Molly was picking up on it, but it was driving Leticia crazy. Every time he looked at her like that, she wanted to spread her legs for him. He would touch her, a quick brush of hands or a tangle of fingers as they reached for the same thing, his fingertips sliding briefly along the inside of her wrist. His leg pressed against hers under the table, making Leticia remember the time in this one restaurant where she'd slid her foot up his leg and between his...

Oh God, this was not appropriate to think about while Molly was in the room. Leticia could feel herself getting a little flushed. She wanted him so badly—but she could wait. She could be patient.

After dinner, Molly wanted them all to play a card game. Carter looked a little unsure, but Leticia said it was fine. If Molly went to bed too early, she suspected they'd be in for some eavesdropping. But if she was nice and tired, she'd genuinely go to sleep and they could have whatever talk they needed to have without Molly overhearing.

And honestly, it was fun. More fun than Leticia had expected. She was a bit competitive when it came to games, but so were Molly and Carter—and they knew this game better than she did. They could get ruthless.

By the time Carter called it quits, citing bedtime and school tomorrow, Leticia was laughing and worn out. Maybe she just hadn't spent this much time around a kid before, but... no, she remembered her younger cousins and her cousins' kids, and knew that this was Molly. She genuinely liked her. There was something special about her—not anything that made her better than any other child, but something that made her fit with Leticia. Something that made the two of them work.

She even hugged Molly goodnight, happy to wrap her arms around the girl and let her hook her chin over Leticia's shoulder. She wasn't super touchy-feely with kids, as a rule, but she wanted to hug Molly. She wanted to feel the girl safe in her arms for a moment.

Carter took Molly up to bed to tuck her in, so Leticia busied herself with cleaning up dinner. It was easy, given that it was takeout, but she took out the trash and wiped up the table and all.

After she'd cleaned up, Leticia just stood there awkwardly, unsure of what to do. Should she sit down at the table? Or maybe go into the living room? Should she get onto her phone or find something else to do so that she didn't look like she was just sitting there waiting like an idiot?

God, she was crap at this. She needed Carter to give her a second chance, and it was making her guts all twist around each other and her heart race until she thought she was going to be sick.

Just at that moment, Carter came down the stairs. He stuck his hands into his pockets, shuffling around a bit. "Hey."

"Hey."

They looked at one another, and it occurred to Leticia that maybe Carter was just as nervous about this as she was. Maybe he, too, wanted a second chance but wasn't sure if she'd want to take it, if she'd want him and Molly both.

The thought strengthened her a little. It helped to know that she wasn't the only one with her heart on the line.

"I'm sorry," she said. "For making things complicated. And not talking to you. But I—I came here because... I want to be with you." She swallowed hard, trying to get over the lump in her throat. "I like Molly. I know I'm not the best with kids but I like her, and I want to try. I really want to try with her. And part of it is because of how I feel for you, but part of it is that I just like who she is. All on her own. She's a great kid."

Carter nodded, a bit of the tension in his body easing out. "I'm not expecting you to be perfect. I didn't start dating you, or dating in general, so I could find someone ready to jump in and be a mom. I know it'll take time."

"But I'm willing to try," Leticia promised. "I'll do my best and I'll do whatever you say is best for her, I promise. I'm not going to just disappear on her. I won't do that to her."

Carter eased his hands out of his pockets and took a step towards her. "You said part of it was how you felt about me."

Leticia felt her face heating up. "Yeah, I... she's a part of you, you know? She's your kid and I can see you when I look at her, and—I love that. Because I..." Oh, to hell with it, she might as well say it. "I love you."

There was a pause, and Leticia thought that maybe she'd gone too far. Maybe she'd been the stupid woman who'd fallen first, far too early, and Carter wasn't... but then Carter let out a huge sigh of relief and strode right up to her, wrapping his arms around her and kissing her.

Leticia clung to him, kissing him back, shivering happily at the feeling of his strong arms holding her tight.

"I love you, too," Carter admitted, the words whispered against her lips. "I want you to be a part of both of our lives."

Leticia wrapped her arms around him, pressing them up against one another completely. "I'd like that. I'd like that a lot."

"Although..." Carter smiled mischievously. "When you stay over, I'd like you to sleep in my room, instead of Molly's."

Leticia laughed. "I think I can be okay with that."

He kissed her again, stealing the laughter from her mouth. "C'mon then," he whispered, and led her up to his bedroom.

Leticia couldn't wipe the stupid smile off of her face for the rest of the night.

EPILOGUE I

*L*eticia sat cross-legged on the floor, completely surrounded by magazine clippings, printed pages from the internet, and booklets. "I'm eloping," she declared. "I give up, I'm eloping, we're just flying out to Tahiti or somewhere and none of you are invited."

"That's the thanks we get for wading through all of this with you?" Melanie asked. She brandished a folder. "How many possible color schemes are there in the world? Huh? Answer me that."

"Oh, shut up. As if you won't be the most panicked bride ever when it's your turn," Leticia shot back.

"How did you manage to plan your wedding, Sharon?" Debbie asked.

Sharon paused in her perusal of appropriate wedding gifts. "Lots of coffee and alcohol," she said finally.

"I shouldn't even be here," Jonas grumbled. "I know I'm gay, but c'mon."

There was a knock at the door. Leticia groaned. "It's open!"

Carter poked his head in. He took in the five of them all sprawled out in the living room and his eyebrows slowly climbed up towards his hairline. "Should I come back later?"

"No, no, you're perfect," Leticia said, dashing up and running over to pull him into the room. She kissed him quickly, giving a little noise of approval when he let his hands drop to her hips. "I needed a distraction."

Carter took in all the planning that was going on. "You know that we can just have something small," he said.

He'd made it clear to Leticia that he didn't care how big or small the wedding was so long as she was happy, but Leticia knew that if she didn't have something big, her family was never going to let her live it down.

"No, it's fine, I just needed a quick break."

"Maybe you can ask Carter what damn flower arrangement he wants," Debbie said.

"Oh thank God, another guy," Jonas gasped, hauling himself to his feet. "Quick, come grab a beer with me, I need to remember I have testosterone."

"You're a goddamn traitor to your tribe, Jonas," Melanie informed him.

Carter obediently let himself be led into the kitchen by Jonas, where they could grab the beers. Carter had met everyone already, but Leticia could tell that he was still getting used to everyone. She wasn't too worried, though—everyone loved him and she'd seen Ross go through something similar when he'd been introduced to them. Carter would find his way into the group in time.

"Don't worry," Sharon said. Leticia looked over at her best friend. The baby, a little girl as Sharon and Ross had hoped, was sleeping peacefully in Sharon's arms. "It'll all work out. Just remember to breathe and that the big day is *your* day, yours and Carter's, not anyone else's, all right?"

Leticia nodded. Right. This was about her and Carter, at the end of the day.

"Hey," she said, "I don't suppose we could do a recreation of the Amber Room, could we?"

Over in the kitchen, Carter spat out his beer.

"The what?" Debbie asked.

"Famous chamber, was in Russia, stolen by the Nazis, never found," Melanie rattled off.

"I'm kidding!" Leticia said, as Jonas patted Carter on the back. "I'm just kidding, yeesh."

"Poor man, you should talk to Ross," Sharon said. "He had to deal with me during our wedding."

Honestly, it was thanks to Sharon that Leticia had all of the information currently strewn all over the floor. She'd saved the big wedding book of files she'd compiled, knowing that her friends would need the information someday, and now they were all going through it to find what Leticia might like.

The problem was that Leticia had no idea what she would like.

Carter smiled at Leticia across the room, and suddenly she knew it would all be okay. She'd figure out what she wanted for the wedding, she'd figure out how to handle all of her insane relatives—whatever was going to come their way, it would be okay. She had Carter and Molly. That was what mattered.

"Oh, God, did Carter hear the story about the Valentine's party junior year?" Debbie asked.

Then again, maybe she was going to make sure Carter never spent any more time around her traitor friends ever.

"I'm sure he doesn't need to—"

"No, go ahead, Debbie, tell me." Carter said. He winked at Leticia, and she relaxed.

She had a guy that put up with her and loved her and enjoyed the crazy stories about her youth and wasn't too fazed by her insane friends. She didn't know how she'd gotten so lucky, but she knew for a fact that she was never letting him go.

EPILOGUE II

*C*arter stood at the altar, trying to calm his nerves.

Everything had been going smoothly. Leticia had finally decided on what she wanted for the wedding, he hadn't offended her family or made an idiot of himself in front of them, and his friends and Leticia's friends were getting along well. Ross and Brian were especially helpful, Brian's bachelor party being the one that had led to Carter meeting Leticia. As his two married friends, they'd counseled him on how to deal with things.

But nothing they had said could prepare him for the moment where he was standing in front of everyone, waiting for Leticia to walk down the aisle, and suddenly hit by the fear that she wouldn't appear.

What if she got cold feet? What if she decided that he wasn't worth her time? What if she realized that she was too much of a free spirit to be with just one person for the rest of her life? What if—

He felt a tug on his shirt sleeve and looked down.

"You're supposed to be in the back!" He whispered.

Molly beamed up at him. She was wearing her adorable, periwinkle blue flower girl dress, which showed off her eyes, and clutching her flower basket to her chest like it was made of gold. "I just wanted to say hi."

"Well, hi, sweetheart, but you have to walk down the aisle."

"Okay." Molly paused. "Letty's nervous."

That made him pause. "Why is she nervous?"

Molly shrugged. "She thinks you're going to change your mind."

Carter almost laughed in relief. Thank God he wasn't the only one standing there thinking his intended was too good for him.

"But don't worry," Molly added. "I told her that you loved her and I loved her and we were already a family, so this was just for fun. To tell people about it."

Carter crouched down, hugging Molly to him. "That was very smart of you to say," he told her. "And I love you. Now seriously, go in the back so you can walk down the aisle."

"Okay." Molly gave him a quick kiss on the cheek and then disappeared.

Carter stood up straight again, and a moment later the music started up. He found himself smiling, his nerves gone.

Molly came down the aisle, sprinkling her flowers very carefully, as if she'd surveyed the aisle beforehand and decided exactly where she was going to drop each flower. Next came the bridesmaids—some cousins of Leticia's, then Debbie, and then Melanie, who was serving as maid of honor since Sharon was married and dealing with a newborn baby.

And then, on her father's arm... was Leticia.

Carter's breath caught in his throat. She was—she was always beautiful, of course, and he'd seen her every day, woken up with her every day, worked with her every day—but it was as if he was truly understanding how beautiful she was for the first time, inside and out.

And she had agreed to marry him.

He couldn't have kept the huge smile off his face if he'd tried. He was going to marry her. Leticia was going to marry him.

He had his daughter, and a new love of his life, and all of his friends and family around him.

This was going to be amazing.

THANK YOU

Just like getting to the happily ever after, the process of publishing this book required creativity, chemistry, open dialogue, many bottles of wine and putting ourselves out there. We hope you enjoyed the final product.

If you liked the **Painted Love** we'd love it if you would be kind enough to take two minutes right now to leave a review. To leave a review simply visit the **book page on Amazon** and click the button that says Write a Customer Review.

If you'd like to read other books by Lacy please sign up at **Lacy-Embers.com**

Thank you for joining us on this adventure!

- The Team Behind Lacy Embers

ABOUT THE AUTHOR

Lacy Embers is a collaboration of authors, writers, and editors who love romance novels. Lacy's novels can be relied upon for steamy romance tropes (billionaires, sports stars, happily ever afters), compelling characters and sexy settings. Her books are best enjoyed with a glass of wine.

To learn more about Lacy Embers please visit **LacyEmbers.com**

www.ingramcontent.com/pod-product-compliance
Lightning Source LLC
Chambersburg PA
CBHW021038130626
46552CB00005B/1904